Legacy

UNSCRIPTED

EJ ST. CLAIRE

For more information, contact: info@ejstclaire.com

ISBN – 979-8-9882286-4-6 (ebook edition)
ISBN – 979-8-9882286-5-3 (print edition)

http://www.ejstclaire.com

 ALQUEMIE PRESS

Contents

Prologue

A little bird told me ...

Well, well, well, dear readers of the Manhattan Herald*!*

Grab your coffee and get ready for a caffeine-fueled ride through the latest juicy gossip of New York City, because it seems Tate Blanchard is about to make his grand entrance into the movie-making scene. And guess what? This isn't just any run-of-the-mill indie movie.

In New York, we always go big or go home, and this time Tate Blanchard is making a full swing with his biopic movie about none other than his late father, Joel Blackwood.

First things first. If you're unfamiliar with Tate Blanchard, what rock have you been living under? The handsome yet single bachelor, one of the Blanchard triplets, has been lurking in the shadows for a while, biding his time and waiting for the right moment to have his five minutes of glory.

His half-sibling Ethan Blackwood, whom we're most familiar with, has been a part of the Manhattan elite for some time, along with his wife Elizabeth, taking a full swing at the tech industry.

The two other siblings who make up Tate's trio of triplets are the beautiful sister—also known as the "former wild child"—Flyn, who is making the covers of every fashion magazine as a model, and his brother, Wade Blanchard, a burgeoning photographer enjoying his recent marriage bliss.

So, what better way for Tate Blanchard to make his claim on fame than banking on being the offspring of the legendary Joel Blackwood? But hey, don't we all need a little nepotism in our lives? If you've got it, flaunt it!

And with his looks, he can charm any big name to join his little project. Haven't you heard who's speculated to be on board already?

Well, it's none other than Vaughn Archer, Hollywood's very own "bad boy." Word on the glamorous streets is that he's been seen in New York City—and not to make trouble it seems.

But picture it. I mean, who else could step into the shoes of a man as notorious as Joel Blackwood? Vaughn Archer has made a name for himself by pushing the envelope and stirring up controversy wherever he goes. It's almost as if he's been training his whole life for this role. And playing a young Joel Blackwood would benefit not only him, but Tate Blanchard himself.

And the leading actresses to pair? Tate seems to have a knack for choosing leading ladies who come with their own share of drama. Newbie Viviana Astor, a no-name in the acting world but a promising rising star, is set to play Marianne Blanchard, Tate's own mother.

Vivi seems to be a recluse, yet she's an Astor and anyone in that family line makes one impact or another. I'm sure we can expect great things. After all, she's also a cousin to the one and only Valesca Astor, who used to be our favorite socialite—at least before she gambled away her luck and ended up on the losing side of the family, getting pregnant with Nathan Valetta's child.

Not to mention rumor has it that their marriage is already on the rocks because of infidelity and they're trying to save their troubled marriage for the sake of their child.

Now that we've dipped our cookie into more bitter coffee, let's talk about Nathan Valletta, the black sheep of the Blackwood family who was not only a no-show at Wade and Wren Blanchard's recent wedding, but it has reached my ears that he and Valesca weren't invited at all.

Was it an oversight, or did he just not make the guest list? Either way, it seems like Nathan's reputation is going further down the drain. Let's not forget his downfall after his online criticism toward the Blanchard triplets following his second failed legal claim to Joel Blackwood's fortune.

Seems to me like Nathan has a knack for stirring the pot with his half-siblings and losing, but if there's one thing we love, it's a good scandal.

Tate's film studio is based in the French Riviera to honor his mother's birthplace, and with the breathtaking views and Mediterranean charm, it is the perfect backdrop for a story as extravagant as Joel Blackwood's. But it's also the current residence of Nathan Valletta and Valesca Astor.

Is Tate provoking Nathan on purpose or is this just some grand coincidence?

It's a gamble to say, but who knows? Maybe Nathan will try to corrupt the filming of his father's movie. Or would he possibly make a dramatic entrance on set, demanding his rightful share of the spotlight?

I'm just dying to know if Nathan would make any more embarrassing headlines for all the wrong reasons once again, or will he surprise us all with a newfound sense of decorum?

Would Tate Blanchard make a name for himself or take the rockier road like his half-sibling Nathan and crash and burn?

Stay tuned and keep your eyes peeled for the next juicy update. Until then, may your lattes be strong and your scandals even stronger!

Resident gossip columnist,

Robin Callahan reporting for the Manhattan Herald

Chapter 1

Tate

The aroma of freshly brewed coffee mingled with the sweet scent of pastries while I waited at the side counter for my coffee order. The bell on top of the door rang when it opened, and a woman walked into the café. Her brown eyes instantly landed on me. The way she looked at me told me she was up for some fun—a challenge I was more than willing to accept. I met her gaze, offering an easy smile, and she returned it, her lips curving like an invitation before telling her coffee order to the barista.

Leaning back casually, I waited for her to walk over. Her heels clicked on the floor as she approached me. "I'm caramel macchiato." A playful spark glinted in her eyes. "You know, for warning, New Yorkers are always in a rush, and there are always some impatient, grabby hands getting my order by mistake."

I chuckled. "I'm iced Americano. I suppose it's not a thrilling drink to steal, but I'll keep an eye out for yours." I glanced at the guy in front of me with a bitter frown on his face. Someone didn't have a nice day. "He looks like he could grab it and make a run for it."

A smile spread on her lips, and she laughed wholeheartedly. In that moment, I knew I had her.

"I'm Tate, and what is your ..." I was about to ask for her name when my back pocket vibrated. I took the phone out, and the screen flashed with an incoming call from my brother. It was about time he called.

"Iced Americano," the barista yelled and placed the coffee on the counter. The guy in front of me yelled after the barista, upset he was waiting longer than I did. I scooped up my coffee and winked at the woman in my company. "Sorry, darling. Duty calls." I raised the phone to my ear. "Enjoy the coffee."

She pouted, obviously disappointed, and I grinned, unable to resist the urge to tease one last time. "Don't worry, sweetness. I come here every day."

She tilted her head, slightly intrigued, slightly taken back by the audacity, but it was part of the charm. Before she could say another word, I walked past her and out of the coffee shop.

"Wade, enjoying your first day back in New York after what I imagine was a very eventful honeymoon in Europe?" I asked, taking a sip from the coffee.

His laugh echoed on the other side of the line. "It was just Italy and France. And we haven't had the chance to do much of anything. You're the first person I called. It's been a slow morning for me and Wren."

The streets were alive with movement. The loud horns of yellow taxis weaved in the background while hundreds of people seemed to pass me by, going on about their busy day, adding to the chaos. As I walked, I looked up at the towering skyscrapers and narrowed my eyes at the blinding sunlight. Unlike my previous apartment, this part of the city was a tapestry of steel and glass, suits with ambitions, and women with long legs. One had to love where they were in life.

"So how was the trip?"

"Oh you know, a little bit of gray, a little bit of color, lots of yelling in languages I don't understand, street art, music, and poor service."

"Aha, tell Wren I want her to do the honeymoon reporting."

I heard him muttering something and then heard her voice in the distance. "Cobblestone streets, ancient castles, breathtaking landscapes, sunsets over charming chateaus, and flower-boxed windows."

"See?" I grinned. "Your wife knows how to enjoy Europe."

I could practically see him roll his eyes. "You can both catch up over dinner. I'm sure she can tell you all about it before you make your way over there. And since we're on the topic, how are things going with the movie?"

In comparison to the previous year, my life had changed tremendously. From living in an almost empty flat and making ends meet with a job I wasn't very proud of to becoming a well-respected movie producer. The dice rolled, and I had my life turned upside down after learning my real father was the late Joel Blackwood. One of the many perks was the financial freedom I got with the inheritance; I was finally fulfilling my dream and doing something meaningful with my life.

"It took us a lot to get there, but it's happening." I couldn't help but proudly smile to myself as I punched in the code for the entrance of my building and took the elevator to my floor. "After a lot of persuasion and personal financial investment, I finally got the green light. The movie about our father and his insane romantic life while climbing the social ladder is going to be a reality."

"Congratulations. It was well earned. I know you worked hard to make it happen."

Unlocking my apartment door, I stepped inside and tossed the keys aside. The chaos was everywhere. My laptop was on the coffee table accompanied by the countless storyboards and ideas I had been working on all night to finish. Scattered on the ground were book volumes of film history, storytelling techniques, and everything I could get my hands on to grasp a proper vision of the story I wanted to tell with this movie. A biopic of my late father, Joel Blackwood, including his love life with a highlight on my late mother.

Wade suddenly got unusually quiet over the phone, one of his many tells when he was overthinking something before bringing it up.

"What?" I placed the coffee down and slumped on the couch. "I know you have something to say."

"I'm glad you're making a name for yourself in the industry and you're putting in effort in this project."

"And time and money," I said.

"But I'm just concerned that you are overly invested in Joel's life. We never even met the man, and if wasn't for Mom telling us he was our father in her will, we never would have known about him."

"But we did. And his inheritance changed everything for us. I got to do movies, and you opened your gallery, and our sister ... well, Flyn never cared about the money, she just got some sort of epiphany after realizing she and Dad were alike. Suddenly all she wanted was to get her life in order, and thank god for that because without Dad we might have lost her."

"Joel," Wade corrected me. "It's weird calling him Dad."

I tilted my head in disagreement. "Ethan would disagree."

"Our half-brother grew up with him, he gets away with it. We grew up with Slade, and I don't like calling him Dad either, as he was gone most of the time and we never really saw him."

"Well, we have two dads, Wade, so we can choose which one we get to call Dad."

"That's not how it works."

"I'm just saying Ethan had it better than us. At least Joel took care of him."

"Just because Wren is a good writer, doesn't mean Joel was a sunshine in Ethan's life either."

Wade's wife Wren had published a book called *Legacy*, a biography of Joel Blackwood going over his most important moments in life like making it in the tech industry and building an empire all while indulging in promiscuous sexual relations in his early days, going as far as getting three women pregnant. That resulted in five children: the triplets, Wade, Flyn, and I; Ethan our half-brother, whom we accepted; and Nathan, another half-brother who, by hating and attempting to ruin Ethan's life by any means in the past, was voted out of the siblings' club by default. I wasn't one to judge people for their mistakes, but turning against family was one thing I couldn't look past.

Ever since I read Joel's biography, something in me clicked. Slade was a hard father to relate to with the absence, the alcohol abuse, and the gambling. Not to mention he wasn't here for our mom when she died of cancer. Chaotic as we were, none of us wanted to go down that road, and none of us liked him either. But reading about Joel was like I understood myself more. He was a person I wanted to know more about.

"Wade, while I appreciate the concern, it's not like I'm not aware he wasn't exactly the father of the year. However, I can't help but be curious. I mean, don't you want to know more about him, the man that could have been our father?"

"Not really."

"Easy to say when Wren probably whispers to you in bed anecdotes she knows about Joel?"

He cackled. "Trust me, the last thing me and Wren do in bed is talk about Joel."

I leaned over to the coffee table, getting my drink. The ice cracked in the cup was almost melted. "I'm doing the movie, and there's nothing you could do to stop me."

He sighed. "Okay, I'm not bringing this up anymore. You can do what you want."

"Thank you."

"So, who do you have on your team so far?"

Wade changed the topic, and I was grateful. I really needed a little bit of support from him on this, especially now that I had a big name on my list. "I got Giles Duval," I bragged.

"No shit." Wade paused in shock. "He is a tough director to get."

"I know." A pleased grin spread across my face. "He will be overseeing the final auditions for actors and actresses next week."

"That's great. Any favorites?"

"I've actually been waiting on that email all morning. I've barely slept, and all I can think about is the final vision I need for this movie. The cast is such a big deal. Just give me a moment."

I took the laptop in my hands and opened my emails. The top one was from Josie, my casting agent.

"I just got the headshots from Josie. She titled the email, '*Do you feel lucky, baby?*' so I'm guessing she is happy about the preliminary auditions."

I scrolled down the email, observing the potential cast.

"Oh shit." I laughed, piquing Wade's interest.

"What?" he asked.

"We have Vaughn Archer as potential Joel. Elena Ricci and Carrie Campbell for Nathan's and Ethan's moms. Wade, these are some great choices, and if Josie likes them, they're probably killers on screen. She doesn't mess around when it comes to stage presence and originality. I'll be making the final call after seeing them next week, but this is good." I took a deep breath. The excitement of running the final lap with this movie project was overwhelming. "This is really good."

"Now I'm curious who is runner-up for our mom."

"Let's see." I scrolled farther down. "The person favored for playing Marianne Blanchard is ..."

My eyes paused on the pictures. There she was, Viviana Astor. A name I hadn't heard before, but it was a face that carried an air of sad beauty. Her headshot occupied the screen, and in that instant, the world around me seemed to blur, leaving only her image.

Her hair, a rich brunette, framed her face in a sleek bob that hinted at a timeless elegance.

"Tate?" Wade's voice echoed on the other side of the line.

Her eyes, a cool blue, held me captive. Deep, almost haunting. They seemed to penetrate the screen and lock onto something within me. There was a sadness in her eyes, one that was tugging on my heartstrings like a piercing violin.

She seemed petite and almost delicate, even in the photo. Yet, there was strength in the way she held herself, a quiet resilience that made her beauty all the more captivating. It was as if every contour of her face, every line around her eyes, held a tale waiting to be told.

As I stared at that photo, I couldn't deny the chill that ran down my spine. There was something about her, something beyond the stunning exterior. Her look was provoking, almost daring, as if she knew she held power over anyone who dared to meet those eyes yet didn't want any of it.

"Tate, hello?" Wade was persistent.

I cleared my throat. "Yeah, um, I don't recognize her, so I guess she's a new talent. Her name is Viviana Astor."

"Haven't heard of her. Wait ..." Wade called out to Wren, asking her if she knew anything about her. Moments later, he was back on the line.

"Wren says she's Rupert Astor's daughter. He used to be a wealthy businessman who died tragically two years ago. The Astors have always been a prestigious family in New York and go back years with their generational wealth and power. One side of the family is very out there, the other side is very lowkey on the social scene. I don't know if you remember Ethan and his wife telling us about the whole fiasco that happened before Joel died?"

"Right, with Ethan's previous fiancé who cheated on him with Nathan and then lied about getting pregnant with Ethan's baby. The same one who had to leave the country with Nathan to avoid the shame."

"That's the one."

"They're related?" I asked.

He paused and then came back on the line. "Wren says the Astor family as a name is influential, but she doesn't think they're very close as a family. Rupert kept his part of the family private. His wife, Colette Astor, also known as Coco, has been running the family for the last two years since Viviana was still young. She is the one managing her as an actor as well. Wren says that's all she knows."

Well, it was more than enough. "Thanks, Wade. I'm going back to work to finish some things. Say thank you to Wren, and see you for dinner."

"All alright, later."

I tossed the phone aside and went back to the headshots. My eyes lingered on the photo with a close-up of Viviana's eyes. One was not to judge someone by his family, I knew that, but I wondered why an heiress who grew up with everything she could possibly want and need had the eyes of a frightened deer waiting to be crushed by the world.

Chapter 2

Vivi

It was a never-ending torture. I stood there, amidst the chaos and bright lights of the set, my heart heavy in my chest. Another photoshoot, another fake smile to plaster on my face, another act to perform. I was acting, even in my day-to-day life, without a break. Everything felt over the top, overwhelming, and suffocating.

As the crew scurried around, setting up the next scene and adjusting lights and backdrop, I felt their eyes on me. Their expectations were hanging in the air like a storm cloud about to burst. They saw a professional, a rising star, someone who had it all together.

Little did they know that every step I took felt like a battle against a living hell. This was too much. I didn't want to do this.

The cameras would click, capturing a moment of supposed joy, while inside, my soul screamed in protest. I was being pushed, forced into these roles and photo ops, a marionette dancing to a tune I couldn't even hear anymore. And if anyone dared to ask, "*Are you okay, Vivi?*" I had to respond with a practiced grin and an affirmative nod. God forbid the press caught wind of any weakness.

I stole a glance at the corner where my mother stood. Colette Astor, or Coco as she was known in the industry, was also my manager, my supposed guiding star.

I could almost laugh about it. More like a tyrant than a mother. She orchestrated my every move, every project, every appearance. The lines between her roles as my parent and manager were blurred beyond recognition.

"Can I take five? I need some air," I asked the girl who was adding an additional layer of blush to my face. I wanted to get out of here.

Uncertain she could make the decision, the girl glanced at the photographer, who was standing with Coco. Suddenly Coco's eyes met mine, and I could see a flicker of the silent command to keep up the act, to play my part without faltering.

"Sorry, never mind." I smiled at the girl and sucked in any complaints.

New clothes were being laid out, each piece more extravagant and elaborate than the last. Minutes later, I was dressed up like a doll, painted in colors that weren't my own, ready to be plastered on another magazine.

"You look stunning, darling. Now pose for me," the photographer instructed me.

I got into my role and then moved when they told me to, posed when they directed me. My body moved on autopilot while my mind drifted into a haze. The burden on my chest grew heavier with each passing second. Just when was this going to be over? I needed the silence, the peace, the dark.

All of this chaos started from the moment Coco realized I could play Marianne Blanchard and I complied. All because of one reason.

"That's it, thank you, darling." The photographer closed the photoshoot, happy with the pictures, and I was escorted by all the make-up artists and hairdressers back into the backroom. Coco was right behind them.

I continued to smile for them, to play my part, while inside, I crumbled. Once it was only Coco and me, she finally exhaled the sigh of disapproval she had been holding all day.

"Seriously, Vivi, if I have to see that frown one more time." She glanced at herself in the mirror, fixing her hair, and then turned back at me. "Do you know how many wrinkles you'll get by keeping that face on?"

"Please, spare me the drama of wrinkles at twenty-one." I grabbed my jeans, tugging them on under the starlet lingerie robe. "I'm going home."

"Home?" She laughed ironically. "You're not going home."

Exhaustion weighed me down like I was carrying a heavy stone. Coco approached with that inscrutable look in her eyes.

"Vivienne, darling," she said with a sweet voice that hid the sharp edge beneath. It was an unsettling blend of sweetness and command. "You have a busy schedule ahead."

I turned to face her, my heart sinking at the thought of what lay ahead. The very mention of my to-do list made my stomach churn.

"I feel like my head will explode if I have to sit through one more of these photoshoots and have to make small talk with people."

"Filming for the movie is set to begin on the French Riviera in a month," Coco continued, her eyes bright with determination. "We need to make sure you're in peak condition for the final audition—physically and mentally. It's almost yours; we just have to secure it."

I was about to tell her that considering the popular actresses in competition for the movie, chances were slim that I would get the role, when Coco grabbed my chin and looked at my face.

"You need to lose a bit more weight," she said casually, as though shedding pounds were as easy as shedding a jacket. "You're going to the gym after this. And after that, I booked some facials for you to ensure you're glowing on screen. And your accent coaching needs to be impeccable. Marianne Blanchard is a complex character, and you need to be convincing."

I tried to mask my misery. "Coco," I began confidently, but my voice quivered. "I don't know if I'm ready for this. The French Riviera, the spotlight ... it's all so much. I'm not saying I won't do acting—just can I please start with something lowkey?"

She turned to me, a calculating glint in her eyes. "Vivi, you have a gift. You were born for this. Remember, you love acting. This is your chance to shine. Why struggle and settle for some side role when you can star in this movie and shoot straight to the top?"

"I love acting, but this role ... it's so high-profile, so intense. I don't know if I can handle it."

She took a step closer, her grip on my arm surprisingly firm.

"Vivienne," her voice lowered to a whisper, "you owe me. After what you put me through ... you owe me."

Tears welled up, and I blinked them back. "But ..."

"Tiredness is a small price to pay considering everything I've done for you. Remember where you were two years ago? Remember who was there to pull you out of that darkness and hide the story from the press? I brought you back into the spotlight, I am the one saving your future and giving you these opportunities, and you owe me for that."

I closed my eyes, my mind flashing back to the hospital room. My father's death had shattered something inside me. The memory of my lowest point came back to haunt me. Like a black hole ready to swallow me again, I took a step back.

My suicide attempt, one of the darkest times in my life, was always her best excuse at a time like this. Coco had swept in like a whirlwind, shoving my pain under the rug, erasing the truth, and propping me up again like a marionette whose strings were firmly in her grip. The worst part of it was that I didn't know if I could even fight her on this, as she was right. She took matters into her own hands while I was at the lowest point of my life, and I had no face to complain. I understood how much I owed her.

My chest tightened. "I ... I'm sorry," I choked out, my voice barely audible. "I just don't want to disappoint you."

She released me, her expression softening just a fraction. "It's not about apologies, dear. It's about fulfilling your destiny. You're going to turn twenty-one in five months, and then your father's trust fund will be yours. But until then, you're under my guidance, as he made sure you'd be before he died."

I wiped away a tear, my resolve crumbling.

Coco's fingers brushed against my cheek. It was such a rare gesture of tenderness. "You won't disappoint me, Vivi. I see the fire in you. Take the pain you feel and channel it into your performance. Marianne Blanchard is tortured, just like you've been."

I nodded, my vision blurred by unshed tears.

A small, victorious smile played on her lips. "That's my girl."

As she left the room, my façade crumbled. Alone once more, I allowed the tears to fall, releasing the pent-up emotions I had been suppressing. I sank to the floor, my sobs echoing in the empty room.

My day after that was a blur. The gym was a haze of clinking weights and pounding footsteps. My body moved on autopilot, muscles burning as I pushed myself through another grueling workout. My limbs moved mechanically, disconnected from the fatigue both mental and physical.

From there, it was off to the facial appointment, where I lay still as someone slathered my face with various potions and lotions. The sweet scents of lavender and chamomile couldn't mask the underlying tension that seemed to follow me everywhere.

Finally, I met with my accent instructor who worked hard for the money she was getting to perfect the nuances of an accent that wasn't mine.

Once I returned home, I filled the bathtub with hot water, the steam rising to my face. I removed my clothes and sunk into the water like my life depended on it. I closed my eyes, allowing the heat to seep into my bones. The weight of the day, the weight of my life, felt momentarily lighter as the water embraced me. But even at this moment, I couldn't shake off the feeling that I was trapped in a life that I had never truly chosen for myself.

The realization that my twenty-first birthday was just around the corner sent a mix of emotions coursing through me. Five months and I would be granted the freedom I so desperately craved.

But until then, I was still bound to Coco. I had to do what she asked.

A shiver ran down my spine as I contemplated the coming months, each day a reminder that I was still under her control, whether I liked it or not. She had plans for me, ambitions that she projected onto me. The role of Marianne Blanchard, the stardom she envisioned for me—it was all part of her grand design, and I had to work hard to fulfill that vision.

Her voice echoed in my mind, a reminder of my debt. Her relentless efforts after my darkest days, the way she'd maneuvered me back into the limelight, all while keeping my pain hidden from the world. It was a debt I couldn't deny, even though it felt like a heavy chain dragging me down.

Coco's words echoed in my head. *"You owe me."*

I closed my eyes, willing the tears that threatened to spill over to stay at bay. The water around me blurred. My life was an act.

As the water cooled around me, I slowly rose from the bath and wrapped myself in a plush robe. I stared at my reflection in the mirror: a face that the world would soon know, yet a person who would remain hidden behind a mask of professionalism.

I wondered what my father would think about this whole thing. His voice echoed in my mind.

"You're a bright child, Vivi," he'd say, his eyes lit up with pride, *"with a world of potential at your feet."*

I traced a finger along the reflection of my lips. The smile felt more like a mask than an expression of genuine happiness.

I closed my eyes, letting his memory wash over me. The late-night conversations over ice cream in the kitchen, the shared laughter of our father-daughter dates, his endless encouragement for all my school activities and ambitions. The fragments of the memories I had of his presence gave me a moment of peace. In the hardest of times, he was the one who'd come to my rescue. He had been my confidant, my mentor, my refuge from a world that often felt overwhelming. His belief in me had been unwavering, and he always supported my dreams.

"Dad," I sobbed, barely keeping my trembling voice still. "Why did you have to leave? How am I supposed to do this without you?"

I opened my eyes, my own reflection staring back at me. The room was silent; the mirror didn't offer an answer. I was alone. No one understood me. I was just a distraction, an entertainment, a means to an end for the people around me. Yet I had no room to complain. Tears didn't rewind time nor were going to save me. I blinked my tears away, taking a deep breath to calm down. *Five more months,* I told myself. Five more months and I'd be free to make choices of my own.

Chapter 3

Tate

I rushed down the hallway until I reached the meeting room. I gripped the door handle and took one breath in preparation. The empty hall was bright by the large window, letting the thin rays of sunshine through over the desks and chairs. The final auditions that could make or break the movie were up next on my agenda, and it all came down to this. My eyes swept across the space.

I noticed the large table set by the window was packed with refreshments, ranging from different beverages to snacks to cater to every person's taste. There were strategically placed flat-screen monitors that lined the room to ensure that every member of our team had a front-row seat to the auditions. The cameras mounted on tripods were ready. Chairs were set, and papers, documents, and pens were over the desk in their designated spot.

I took another deep breath to calm my excitement. I was usually calm, but I suddenly felt the upcoming anxiety as I waited for the director, Giles, and casting agent, Josie, to join me. The final auditions meant the project would be realized soon and everything I worked so hard for would become a reality. The doors opened, and Giles walked in first.

He was tall and lean, and barely anyone could tell he was a man in his early fifties. He strode into the room with an air of seasoned confidence, which he probably gained from years of honing his craft and building a respectable image and reputation in this business. His attire spoke for him. He wore a charcoal-gray suit with a white-collar jacket underneath that brought out a blend of artistic flair and practicality. The absence of a tie seemed deliberate, as his whole look was carefully styled yet intentionally tousled.

He extended his hand, taking mine in a firm grip.

"Giles."

"Tate."

"Let's get this show on the road, shall we?"

I flashed him a smile, returning the grip on his hand. "Absolutely."

His gaze swept across the room, taking in the audition setup. There was curiosity in his expression, a hunger to see how the pieces of this puzzle would come together. He was judging every step of the process, observing my moves, and making an assessment of my work ethic style and personality. But I was well prepared for this, and I was certain I could impress him.

I turned toward Josie, putting an arm around her shoulder, a sign of friendly affection she was used to. "Tell me everything is set for the final auditions."

"Baby, I will blow your mind." She tapped my chest and flashed me a smile to calm me down.

Josie was a professional who had a way with people. She knew for me to be my best self, she had to keep panic and anxiety out of the way, so as always, she shamelessly flirted. Her persona changed based on what people needed, but I wasn't sure even that helped.

"Don't tease me, Josie. This man is not just a director. He's a storyteller, a visionary, and I need him to make this movie a success."

She smiled at me flirtatiously. "He's already on board, and he's here to help you choose the perfect match for this movie. Did you see our favorites?"

"I did."

"Good. Let's take a seat. I'll give you a rundown on the finalists as they arrive."

The moment she walked away, her heels clicked on the floor with confidence. It was evident in her stride that she was a powerhouse when it came to her work. Her posture was impeccable—shoulders squared, back straight—exuding a sense of command that came from knowing her industry inside out.

There was always a playful glint in her eyes that revealed how comfortable she was in her place. It was a way of easily acquiring connections, of drawing people in, and it was all done with the kind of finesse that only came from years of experience.

Her wife must have been proud.

I took a deep breath and followed her. I had put my trust in the team I chose, so I walked after her, a bit more at ease.

Some time later, the actors started arriving one by one, and then as we called them, they set foot in the center for their final auditions. The ones that had left the biggest impression on Giles and Josie stood out from the start.

Carrie Campbell was an already seasoned actress who had a reputation for being punctual, dedicated, and prepared for a role, and she made it known today. Halfway through her audition, I already knew she was the perfect fit to play Ethan's mom. The resemblance was there too from pictures I'd seen. She was tall with dark hair cascading down to her waist in sleek waves, framing her face in a way that accentuated her features. The sharpness to her face, the wide eyes, and the flirty look added a flair of the classic American beauty of the 80s.

Right after her was Elena Ricci to play Nathan's mom. Elena Ricci walked to the center stage in effortless glamour. She was a typical Hollywood starlet with famous parents, but despite being in her mid-twenties with not as many experiences, Elena possessed the *it* factor for this role.

Her sun-kissed complexion and curly dark hair that fell around her shoulders displayed typical Italian beauty, and she wore diamond-studded earrings, drawing our eyes to her face. She was calculated and knew what was needed for the role as she finished her audition. She was as good as any in my book.

Lastly, it was time for the actresses who were supposed to play my mother's role—Marianne Blanchard. I was going to be a harsh critic considering I wanted the cast for my mother to be as good a fit as the rest of them. I carefully observed them one by one until I finally got to Viviana.

Josie nudged my side. "She is the one I told you about."

I was about to say something when she came to the center of the room, and my words got stuck in my throat. I couldn't believe the hold she had on me even away from her picture. She was already in costume, one of my mother's outfits that she wore in one of the movies she starred in. The resemblance was uncanny.

Even before she spoke her lines, her presence commanded attention. The whole room was silent for her performance.

She suddenly locked eyes with me. Deep-set, almond, blue eyes stared into mine for a few seconds. They glinted as if they were on the verge of breaking into tears.

Was it stage fright? Nerves? Had she always had that vulnerable look to her?

She looked shorter and more fragile in person. Her round shoulders were covered with the short-sleeved, floral sun dress while her neckline was delicately bare. The pink dress was cinched in her waist, revealing her slim figure.

Staring at her for too long seemed to make her tense up. She looked away, tucked a short strand of her hair behind her ear, and then gave herself a second before snapping into the role.

I still couldn't look away even if it wasn't my job to watch her. Her makeup accentuated her natural features, particularly her eyes. She wore a subtle hint of earthy tones on her eyelids and a sweep of mascara to draw attention to her expressive gaze and red lips—a touch of detail that seemed to be working. I couldn't look away. She looked like a warm autumn sunset.

As the auditions began, I braced myself for the wave of emotions that I knew would come. She started, and I was instantly captivated. The vulnerability in her eyes conveyed more depth and feeling than the very lines could. The scene she did was a part of the script we gave her for the ending. Watching her play that part was both mesmerizing and heart-wrenching.

As she finished the performance, the room was quiet. Josie snapped out of it first and then thanked her for her performance before she walked away.

She turned to me. "You liked her too, I can tell."

I got my shit together and turned to her, relaxing back in my seat. "Just because I liked her performance doesn't mean she is the perfect fit. There are many factors at play here."

She shrugged, disappointed in my answer. "Well, the call is yours, but you can't deny what you see. She has talent."

She was right there.

Giles leaned back in his chair, overhearing the whispered conversation. "I think she's a fine actress too."

I sighed. Before we rushed into things, there was one more thing to take into consideration. "What worries me is her management. I heard her mother is the manager."

Giles took a paper and brought it by the side of his face to hide that he was about to gossip. "She's under the full control of her mother until she's twenty-one, following her father's death two years ago. I've heard Coco has a hard-nosed reputation."

"See, sounds like a problem, and I don't want problems in this movie." I crossed my arms.

Josie took a pen and tapped it over the table to get my attention. "Everyone knows Vivi's one to watch. What if someone decided to swipe her under our noses and take her to LA? We have to be smart, boys."

I tilted my head to the side, unsure if this was the direction I wanted to take. She was perfect for the role, but my gut was reacting to her in some sort of way, and I didn't want to take a chance on something I was unsure about. This movie meant a deal more to me to just risk things as I usually did.

Next in line was Vaughn Archer, a name that carried both promise and controversy, and he was auditioning for the role of Joel. I already had my sights on him from the start, and I hated to say my mind was already made up. He was standing around six feet tall exactly like Joel, and he had an imposing presence just as I'd seen in videos that Joel had. He ran his fingers through his dark hair, a smug smile plastered on his face, confident the role was already his. The audition began, and Josie and Giles observed him carefully.

Giles and Josie didn't seem too happy about him. Vaughn had a reputation as an incredible actor but was matched by his notoriety for being a bit of a bad boy. And I took it that was the nice way of putting it.

But Vaughn's potential to embody Joel was too great. Even with his attitude, he made a perfect fit for Joel. As he delivered the last of his lines, Vaughn's intensity captivated everyone. His raw performance with improvisation and the willingness to expose the flawed nature of the character were exactly what I wanted.

But I couldn't ignore the skepticism etched on Giles and Josie's faces.

"What worries us?" I asked them.

Giles raises an eyebrow, his expression a mix of amusement and concern. "His reputation first and last."

"Is exactly what makes him perfect for the role," I tried to convince. "Joel isn't a straightforward character. He's flawed, unpredictable, and fiercely himself. Vaughn's got all of that."

Josie's eyes narrowed as she considered my words, and then she smiled as if she'd found my weak spot. "Look, I understand that, but his reputation is still a risk. If you're going to defend him as a risk because of the talent, then you can't be hard on Vivi just because of her mother."

Vaughn, who'd been silently observing our debate, suddenly came closer and leaned over the table confidently. "I can tell you're discussing things you've heard about me, but I'm serious about this movie."

"We're also looking to see if you fit with our other actresses." Josie took a document and gently nudged Vaughn off the desk with it. "Now if you'll excuse us."

"Tell you what, if Vivi gets the part of Marianne, I'll play Joel, and I'll play him as you want. I find the idea of us being your parents kind of amusing. I mean, we're both in our early twenties and you're, what, like thirty?" His lips curve into a smirk. There was mischief in his eyes, wanting to see what the provocations would do.

I saw now what they meant by a nasty attitude. But if it got me what I wanted ... "I just turned twenty-seven. In that case, how about you let the grown-ups make a decision." I quickly followed it up with a laugh to soften the blow. "I'm just joking. Good to know you have enthusiasm for the role."

He didn't seem to appreciate getting brushed off, but he tucked his tail under and walked away.

Giles and Josie were mortified by his behavior. Before they argued, I raised my hand and spoke. "The offer he's putting on the table is intriguing and, let's be honest, having Vaughn attached could be a major boost for the film."

They couldn't argue with that.

"So do we have our cast?" I asked excitedly.

Josie and Giles gave it a final thought and then both nodded in approval. It was showtime.

Chapter 4

Vivi

Sunlight filtered through the curtains, casting a subdued glow across the living room over the golden-colored Persian rug, the hardwood floor, and bouncing off the white furniture of my home.

The apartment I lived in was on one of Manhattan's most prestigious blocks, an Upper East Side mansion, dating back to the Gilded Age. It was an inheritance my grandfather left to my father that would in five months belong to me.

Back when I was young, guests visiting worshiped this place. They would compliment the garden, the entertaining spaces, the wood-paneled walls, or the intricate moldings. Everything was a sight, from the classical white columns to the large bay windows.

The home was beautiful, and the historical touch always drew the guests in. Everyone would have a magical experience.

Since two years ago, this home had turned from an array of colors to a home of ghosts. The rooms that were once filled with activities and laughter were now painfully quiet.

I sat in the plush armchair, the lemon-hued silk of my dress contrasting softly against the white backdrop. The material whispered against my skin as I brought my legs up on the armchair, focusing on finishing the page of the book I was reading instead of the past. I pinned back a short strand of hair behind my ear and then turned the next page. I stared at a paragraph for a full minute until I realized I wasn't reading the words.

The hum of subtle activity surrounded me as the staff moved with practiced efficiency. They tidied the room with a silent understanding of my mood. Despite being two years since my father's passing, the weight of his absence clung to every corner of our home, and it might have partially been my fault.

As I absently traced a finger along the rim of a porcelain teacup on the side table, a gentle voice broke through the silence. It was Alice, one of the housekeepers my father had employed.

"For you, Miss Vivi," she said, her lips curving into a small smile. "A little something to brighten your day."

She approached with a plate in hand, a single cookie resting upon it. Her eyes held the warmth and compassion of a friend who understood what I was going through. She was one of the oldest employees here and had served me since I was a little girl.

I managed a soft smile in return, accepting the cookie with gratitude. "Thank you, Alice."

Alice lingered for a moment. "And don't you worry, Miss Vivi," she said in a hushed tone, leaning closer. "I'll make sure to keep this little treat between us. No need to trouble your mother with such things. One cookie will not make you fat."

Her words elicited a genuine chuckle from me. Alice's loyalty was a cherished treasure, that was for sure.

As Alice retreated to her tasks, my gaze traveled to the door of the living room as one of the staff carried in a vase with fresh flowers.

Right after him entered our butler. "Miss Vivi, you look beautiful today," Denis exclaimed in his warm tone as he entered the room carrying today's mail and what was left of the paper we received these days. Most were invitations to parties and other events where Coco could spend money.

"Thank you, Denis." A smile curved on my lips. He complimented me so often that sometimes it felt more like politeness than the truth, but it was the only conversation we were able to have these days, so I was grateful. After what happened, everyone was tiptoeing around me.

I made sure they never forgot my father's death, and Coco never let them forget what I did because of it.

I closed the book and enjoyed the cookie in silence. This home was everything to me; every nook and cranny reminded me of my father, and it was the only thing I never let Coco touch and change.

I got up and walked barefoot through the house. The aimless walk took me to the top floor, and I roamed the rooms that were reserved for guests but we barely used anymore. This house was empty and sad, and the more time passed, the more abandoned it seemed.

"Vivi!" Coco's loud voice brought me out of my trance. She was yelling after me from downstairs.

"She's upstairs, ma'am," Alice answered her.

"Oh, for fuck's sake," I heard her answer, and a minute later, she was up on the top floor with me. She carried something in her hand that seemed like a contract.

Oh no.

"Vivi!" she exclaimed as she saw me, and she rushed over, hugging me. "The role is yours! You have it."

I stood there as she hugged me. "I got it?"

"What's with the face?" Coco's voice was laced with confusion. "You got the part you auditioned for! We're going to the French Riviera in three weeks! Can't you be a little more excited?"

My heart sank further. I wanted to be excited, but the last thing I wanted was to be in the spotlight, to pretend that everything was fine when it was far from it. "I, um ... I don't want the role, Coco," I muttered. "I thought I could do it, but I can't."

Coco's smile faltered. "Why not? We've been over this. This could be a wonderful opportunity for you, a chance to become famous."

I averted my gaze, my fingers tracing up and down my arm. "I'm sorry."

"No." She cut right to the point. "You're doing this. We've been over this."

I took a step closer to her. "Coco, please. I'll pay you back some other way. I don't want to do this."

"No." She was persistent. "This is not a valid reason."

"I ..." I tried to think of another reason, and a memory resurfaced. "Tate, the director! I don't like him."

The truth was he left an impression on me—one I couldn't ignore, no matter how forcefully I pushed against it.

Tate, with his tall frame and striking blond hair, was more the embodiment of a classic leading man rather than a director. His blue eyes set him apart. They were deep and provoking, like windows into a world very different from mine.

He looked at me with a stunned admiration. Men always locked their gaze on my face, my body ... I could see it on their expressions, the thoughts that ran through their head. But his gaze scratched beyond the surface, and it was unsettling. I felt exposed and vulnerable under his gaze.

There was a moment at the audition when our eyes met and I felt that spark. It ignited something within me that I hadn't felt in a long time. And even though I tried to shake off the memory, his face resurfaced time and again. So I decided to deal with it the only way I knew how. To hate him.

"I don't like him. There, I said it!"

Coco snorted in shock. "You're not famous enough to be choosey of directors. If you want to choose directors in the future, then better get to work and sign this contract."

"But ..."

"And be nice to him." She pointed a finger at me like she was threatening me rather than giving me a piece of advice. "He's making a movie as a tribute to his late father. You, of all people, should understand the pain of losing a father. Bond with him."

Frustration bubbled up inside me. " I don't want to do it! How can I stand in front of the world and pretend to be someone else when I'm still struggling to cope with who I've lost?"

I refused to back down this time. Coco's grip tightened over the contract in hand.

"Vivi," Coco tried to calm down. "You need to get out of your comfort zone. I'm telling you this for your own good."

I shook my head, standing my ground. "I won't sign it."

Coco's patience snapped. "You're acting like a spoiled brat." She grabbed my arm and then pushed me into one of the guest rooms then swung the door shut. "Then you'll get treated as one."

I reached for the doorknob, but the door didn't budge. I heard her lock it from the outside.

"Coco! What are you doing? Let me out!" I screamed.

"You'll stay in there until you come to your senses. You're taking this role, and you better learn to like it."

"Why are you doing this?"

"You're lost. You need help. You can't think for yourself. I'm doing this for your own good. You will thank me eventually."

"Open this door!" I shouted, I screamed, I pounded my fists against the door, but I knew it was futile. She wouldn't release me until I yielded to her will and signed that contract.

I sank to the floor, tears streamed down my face. A headache was starting to pound in my temples. Was I really lost? Did I need help? As the chaos in my head was set free once again, I began doubting my own decisions.

Chapter 5

Tate

"Hey, ugly," I greeted Flyn as soon as she opened the door to her apartment.

She swung her arm around my neck and tried to pull me down. "You brat. Did I not tell you I'll kick you in the balls if you call me ugly?"

I tackled her until she staggered backward in the apartment and finally called it a truce.

She pushed her hair back and took a breath. "Take a seat."

I glanced around the apartment. A year ago, this place looked like a whore house, with underwear everywhere—both hers and others—drugs, and empty bottles of alcohol. Now it looked like a completely different apartment. She had renovated it to fit her style as a fresh beginning after getting her life in order and doing great in rehab. I was proud of her for doing so, and despite the event of her overdose being scary and something I didn't ever want to experience again, we were closer now more than ever.

She looked more beautiful every time I saw her, she was taking proper modeling jobs now, and she had gained more respect in the industry. There were some of Wade's photography work on her walls and shelves.

"Don't worry." She caught me staring and smiled. "I've saved this frame ..." she walked over to the shelf that had one empty photo frame on it, "for when I walk the red carpet on your movie premiere."

The very thought of her thinking that far for me made my whole chest swell with warmth and pride. I couldn't let her know that though.

"What is this? For me?" I sat down on the couch, looking at the coffee table that had all sorts of snacks and a large iced coffee for me on it. I reached out for one of the chocolate cookies.

"Yes, I baked those cookies," she replied, sitting down.

I coughed the cookie right out. "You should have warned me sooner."

"Why?" She reached for a cookie. "What's wrong with them this time? I made sure I didn't forget the sugar this time." She put one in her mouth and then shot me a glare. "You asshole, they taste fine."

I shoved the cookie back in and smiled with a full mouth. "Oops."

"So, what's going on with the movie? Did you get your dream cast?"

I dusted off my hands from the crumbs. "Yeah. We made the final call, but they have yet to sign the contracts."

"Well, it's a matter of time now."

"Yep." I stretched my back and leaned on the couch.

"Who do you have so far?"

I raised my hands. "Giles to direct it, Vaughn Archer as Joel."

She gasped. "The bad boy? Isn't he hard to work with? I heard he got into a physical fight with one of the other actors in his drama series and they gave him the boot."

I responded with a nonchalant shrug, making a wavering motion in the air with my hand. "I mean, eh. He is an asshole, I can tell you that much, tried to provoke me from the start, but I can deal with him. I like his acting. He makes a good Joel?"

She smirked. "Reckless."

"Immensely."

"Sexy?"

"Had the leading actresses' vote to cast him. They all had good chemistry with him."

"If he can charm the women, then I approve of him playing Joel. Our father was an immense flirt from what I've read in Wren's book, and Ethan told me that he caught Joel once with his last wife doing it on a bungee swing in his backyard. Can you imagine at his age?" She laughed. "He makes me so proud."

I laughed. "I can't believe Ethan told you that."

"We were bonding over traumas, and he slipped." She took another cookie from the table. "Who else did you get?"

I leaned back on the couch. "Elena Ricci as Nathan's mom, Carrie Campbell as Ethan's, and Viviana Astor as our mom. It's a good cast overall."

Out of nowhere, a sad smile curved on Flyn's face. "Lucky you. Both of them are hot too. And then you're off to the French Riviera." She sighed. "How nice."

I gave it a thought. After her rehab, Wade and I spent every moment of our free time with Flyn to make sure she was okay. The checkups turned into regular sibling dates, and now we were close enough to do dinners and lunches on a weekly basis. But these past couple of months, both of us had less and less time to see her, and I could tell she was getting lonely. The once prideful Flyn was making it a lot more obvious she wanted us around.

Before I knew it, I had made a decision. "Why don't you come with me then?"

She narrowed her eyes and smiled in disbelief. "What?"

"Come with me to Europe." I leaned forward, taking out my phone. "Want me to book you a ticket now?"

"Are you crazy? You're going there to shoot a movie, not for vacation."

I shrugged. "It's a movie about romance and our mom and dad. You will enjoy it. I'll even allow you to criticize my portrayal of their lives."

She shook her head. "It's not my style to judge."

"Come on." I urged her. "The beach, the sun ... we can hang out in my free time."

It didn't take much to change her mind. I could see it in her eyes that she wanted to come. One last swing and she was in.

"I heard the best of the best go there. Who knows, maybe love will bloom?"

She fell over on the couch laughing. "Sold!"

I laughed. "I knew I had you there."

"I want love." She sighed with a smile on her face. "I see Wade and Wren, and I get jealous."

I knew exactly what she meant. "He's got it pretty good. And if he managed to get married with his personality, then there must be hope for us."

"You're absolutely right," she said. "I guess the French Riviera could be my lucky break. What about you? Any lovers you have to part with, or are you planning on screwing every European with sexy legs you see?"

I raised my hands. "I have standards too, you know."

"Aha." She rolled her eyes.

"But as you said, I'm not there for vacation, so between the movie and dealing with the whole crew there, unless romance blooms with someone from the leading ladies, I doubt I'd get laid."

Flyn raised her coffee glass. "To abstinence, whores, and sandy shores."

I clinked her coffee glass with mine. "Cheers."

* * *

I was finishing up some of my work in the studio when I heard heels click outside in the hallway. Everyone was done for the day, and most of the lights were already down. The only one who stayed this late was Josie, but I had seen her leave earlier today to get some last-minute things done before our trip. I placed the documents down and waited for the person to show up at my door.

Leaning on the doorframe was an unfamiliar woman.

The lights in my office were dimmed, casting a soft, almost intimate glow across the room. The faint hum of the air conditioning was the only sound.

I let my gaze linger on hers for a few seconds before realizing why she was actually here.

She was ten years older than me, but it wasn't the first time I'd had an older woman taking the clothes off me with her eyes and wanting me to do the same to her with my hands.

Her straight hair was down falling over the silk shirt she wore that already revealed a lot of what lay beneath. The tightness of her skirt clung to her hips, a very devious touch of sensuality to play on her curves. She was here this late for a reason, and making it very obvious too.

"Who are you?"

"Someone who will be joining you in Europe soon. We haven't met officially yet," she answered with a sultry tone.

"I haven't met the rest of the team coming to Europe. Which team do you belong to? Cameraman?" I took a good look at her. "Stylist?"

"Agent," she answered and took a step inside the room. "But that's not important."

"What brings you here this late?"

She walked the rest of the way to my desk. "I was dropping off a signed contract. I wasn't sure how urgent it was, so I decided it was best to hand deliver it."

She placed her hands over my table and leaned slightly. Her silk shirt hung loosely, leaving little to the imagination. After a sneak peak of her black lace lingerie, she straightened her back and then walked around the office, taking a look at the rather plain space. "I see you still haven't added your personal touch. I can recommend a designer to do some interior work here. You know, image is everything." She glanced back at me. "After we're back from Europe, of course."

I rose from the chair and circled the desk, leaning on it. "Who are you managing, and why do you need to be there?"

"You need me there. My actor needs management and guidance."

Was she referring to Vaughn? I thought his agent was a man.

She approached me carefully like a skilled lioness approaching her prey. When she finally reached me, her fingers wrapped around the first button on my shirt, playing with it.

I took her hand and removed it. "I am flattered."

"Why?" She tilted her head. "I haven't done anything for you to feel flattered."

"It's pretty late already."

Did she want to sleep with me in order to get her actor more screen time or something? But if she was managing Vaughn, then there would be no need for that. Maybe she wanted to do damage control beforehand as he was known to be troublesome.

"There is no need for this."

"I'm not doing this for anyone else. I am doing this because I want this." She took her hand out of mine and continued unbuttoning my shirt. "And I always get what I want."

"I don't want problems," I told her. "Can you keep your actor in line?"

She smirked and leaned even closer. "I can handle people."

Her perfume lingered under my nose, a strong citrusy combination that grazed my senses and overwhelmed me. I didn't like aggressive women coming onto me no matter how much of a skilled lover they were.

I grabbed her hands again, stopping her, but she expertly took her hand out and then grabbed my cock over my pants. Her long-nailed manicured hand began stroking it. "I'm also good at handling other things"

She tilted her head traced her tongue over my lower lip while grinding over my cock. I got hard after few strokes, my resolution faltering.

Fatigue had built up through these whole months' long preparation process, and it had been a while since I last took my frustration out in sex. A little meaningless fucking wouldn't be so bad.

Lips crashed, tongues intertwined. The kiss was fierce and demanding from the get-go. I grabbed her and pressed her onto the table. She reached behind, pushing things aside and then sat on it, spreading her legs for me.

I pushed her skirt farther up her thighs in a frenzied need to get on with it faster.

"Nobody is coming back to the office, right?" she asked.

I tossed her shirt off, revealing the black, lacy bra underneath. "We're alone for the night. Don't worry."

"Oh, I'm not worried. I perform well even with a crowd."

"That's something we have in common," I muttered without thinking too much.

She kept herself busy with my belt while I yanked down her bra and cupped one of her large breasts. Her nipples, a darker shade of brown, were already perked up. I took one of them in my mouth, and her body instantly reacted.

Both my hands roamed around her breasts for a while as I switched sides, sucking her nipples.

"I want to be fucked right now," she moaned and ran her fingers through my hair.

It was all the motivation I needed. I pushed my pants down to my knees and took my hard cock in my hand. I slipped a condom on and stroke my cock in front of her.

I loved how easy fucking someone was. When you're a virgin, the whole ordeal looks so complicated and slow. In reality, the easiest thing in the world was to take off your clothes and then let someone take you on a pleasure ride. It numbed all the darkest thoughts in your head like any good vice could.

I took pleasure in fucking even if I barely knew the person I was inside. My body had been used to the empty but satisfying pleasure for years now.

I watched her spread her legs for me again, watching me in delight, and then she brought her hands down on her clit, playing with herself.

"I heard you were a porn star before," she suddenly said.

There it was. My shameful past was thrown into my face. I felt my blood run cold as she said it. I didn't expect it to be a secret, but I didn't think someone would find out this soon. I had no regrets, as I did what I had to do in the past, but I had spent a good amount of money to keep it a secret until I got my film business going.

Of course, it would take someone with a great deal of money to do some digging to find that out. As if it was a game, she smiled.

Did she want to threaten me? Tease me?

"Where did you hear that?" I asked.

"Just somewhere." She smirked and then tilted her head in a teasing way. "That's not important at all, baby. All I want to know is if you can fuck as a good one?"

Her choice of words threw me off, but I was at this point too horny to care, and as she said, she wanted to know if I could fuck like one.

A grin spread across my face. "I can show you. Do you want foreplay?"

She smirked as if it was provocation. "I'd rather we just get right on it."

"You got it." I pressed my tip at her entrance, getting it wet, and then shoved half of my length in her.

"This feels so amazing." She clenched her hands around my biceps while her pussy gripped my cock. "I can already tell it's going to be good."

She grabbed me by my neck for a kiss and then took the rest of me in her. Her pace was quick, but she was incredibly tight around me. I placed my hand on her throat and then wrapped my fingers around it. Her eyes, a deep unsettling blue, dared me to go for it.

I squeezed a tighter grip on her throat and then kept thrusting in her. Her moans turned into desperate grunts as she moved up and down my cock at a faster pace. Her hips moved on her own, and she wasn't letting the pace drop.

The woman knew how to ride. I watched her take me in and out of her, my cock pressing against her clit with each stroke.

I knew she'd be a great fuck. The simple act of fucking was as old as time, and nothing was more fun than watching a woman climax on your cock.

Once we were finished fucking and she was getting dressed did I finally asked the important question.

"What did you say your name was?"

She put on her bra and fixed the strap before turning toward me. "Coco Astor. I'm managing Vivi."

Chapter 6

Tate

Three weeks later. French Riviera, France.

I stood at the edge of the patio and leaned over the wrought iron rail, taking in the breathtaking view that stretched before me. The villa my team and I rented was nestled into the sun-kissed hillside of the French Riviera.

It was an elegant, white, stone house with a style reminiscent of a graceful era that had passed. Mom would have loved it.

The villa, just like she had been, was a vision of timeless beauty. And it was the perfect setting for everyone to settle in while we were shooting the movie. The actors and most of the crew seemed to be pretty happy with my choice too.

We were a small group, but I had everything I needed to make this movie a success.

The villa's position was nothing short of perfection. I could see the Mediterranean Sea glistening under the long sky, stretching endlessly into the horizon. The mountain range stood sentinel on the opposite side, its rugged peaks painted in hues of earthy brown, dusky pink, and burnt orange, contrasting with the blue sea below. It would look great on camera during sunset.

The cobblestone paths around the villa were decorated with bursts of lavender and rosemary. Large palm trees cast shadows over it.

The villa was surrounded by gardens that seemed to intertwine with colors, roses in various shades of red and pink. The flowery scent lingered gently in the breeze.

The villa's whitewashed stone facade had Bougainvillea climbing the walls, the vivid magenta petals contrasting against the pristine white. Wooden shutters adorned the windows, their soft blue hue depicting the Mediterranean sky above.

The stone pathway led to the summer kitchen, with walls painted in a soft pastel. The kitchen was shaded by a pergola draped with wisteria. A long, rustic, wooden table stood at its center, soft white furniture around it. Nearby, a pool shimmered, and beyond that was the equally impressive guest house and tennis court.

My god. I took a second to take a deep breath. It was better than I had imagined.

I walked inside the villa first, a few others following behind me. Vaughn had stayed outside to smoke, Carrie and Elena— already used to these sorts of views—went straight upstairs to get to a room of their choosing, and the rest of the staff either made themselves comfortable in the space or scattered around to take in the views.

The villa's interior was as elegant and refined as the outside. It blended traditional Provençal elements with modern comforts seamlessly. Sunlight poured through tall French doors, casting a warm glow over the polished floors.

The walls were in muted tones of cream and sage. In the living room, there was a carved grand fireplace of local stone, but the rest of the room was plush sofas and armchairs. I never planned for indoor shoots here, but now that I took a good look at it, I could definitely see a scene or two in this room.

I was still trying to get used to the sights, trying my best not to show how overwhelmed I was. I needed to keep my composure in front of the cast and crew and not let them know I was only a commoner before my late father's inheritance.

Renting this villa was more than me just spending money on luxury. I needed all the arsenal at my disposal to create a great movie and pay tribute to my father.

For a split second, while I was in thought, Vivi passed me and stood a few steps farther. She seemed to glide past me with an effortless grace that made her appear as though she were part of the villa.

My eyes locked on her profile.

A gorgeous woman always made an impact. But this one had a regal air to her like she had stepped right out of a classic movie, like the ones I had watched with my mother growing up, making me fall in love with the art of moving pictures. She seamlessly integrated into this setting. Meanwhile, I felt like an outsider, out of place. How many years of wealth and power would I need to feel like I belonged?

Appearances didn't matter much to me before, and my reputation was already smudged with my previous career choices. But I didn't like how out of place I felt next to a woman who, for some reason, I wanted to look good for.

Vivi had a face that carried an effortless, simple, but flawless beauty. However, her demeanor, like the first time I had seen her, was cold and unapproachable.

And then her eyes caught onto something on the other side of the room, and I saw it. A fleeting glimpse of sadness in her eyes was lurking under her stiff demeanor.

Was she worried about something? Did I misinterpret her icy demeanor?

She had refused to talk to anyone since arriving, and no matter the attempt, she brushed off everyone one by one until no one bothered her. Maybe it was nerves or something else, but it only fueled my curiosity.

"Are you excited?" I flashed my charming smile and waited for her to turn.

She snapped her head at me, and then her expression shifted abruptly. Her softness was replaced by an icy glare, and her demeanor became distant and unyielding.

She let out an irritated sigh, disgusted with me, and then without saying a word, she turned on her heel and headed upstairs, her footsteps fading softly on the villa's stairs.

A gnawing feeling started eating away at me. Did she know I slept with her mother? Once I heard the name "Coco Astor" leaving that woman's lips, I knew I had made a horrible mistake. But how was I supposed to know that was her mother?

Coco wasn't that old, and Vivi was almost twenty-one. How young was Coco when she had Vivi? Something was out of place here.

Then Coco's words replayed in my head. Didn't she say her actor was problematic? Was it possible that I was wrong about her and she was just another snobby brat like her cousin Valesca?

A snort left my lips before I knew it. I had a movie to shoot; it was probably best for me to stay away from the Astor women.

I gripped the strap of my bag, yanking it farther up on my shoulder, and then I left to find a room.

* * *

Later that evening, I gathered everyone in the summer kitchen, throwing a welcome party and letting everyone get to know each other.

Drinks were served, alcohol poured into everyone's bloodstream, and the setting sun did my job for me of relaxing everyone and having them ease into the conversations.

The actors and the rest of the staff seemed to hit it off pretty well; everyone was happy with the house, they were more than motivated to film the first scenes of the movie in the designated locations in and near this villa, and I was becoming more confident that this movie was starting off on a good note. After a good couple of cocktails, Vaughn had taken it upon himself to entertain the actresses by doing impressions and telling some of his surfing stories that I didn't believe that much.

I ambled by the length of the pool to the other side of the villa to join Josie and Giles when I spotted Vivi by the rail, staring at the already dark sea and the barely visible blue shades in the sky, her face illuminated in the afterglow of the rising moon.

I remembered her reaction to me this morning and how annoyed I was, but my body responded to her despite my logical reasoning.

Aloof as always, she was alone and avoided talking to anyone from the cast or staff. She had her arms wrapped around her bare shoulders, shielding herself from the chill in the breeze, enveloped by the quiet on this side of the villa.

Coco's words about Vivi—that she was difficult—resonated in my head. Did Vivi believe just because she was an Astor, she was better than us? That the staff and the rest were beneath her level, therefore she couldn't waste her time entertaining a crowd like us? Like me?

Despite it, my body ached to approach her. I said I would stay away from Astor women, so what the fuck was I doing?

I had managed to avoid Coco Astor all day, but thanks to that, I didn't know if Vivi's behavior was her own or because she hated me in particular.

Everything pointed to the idea that little Miss *"spoiled by her wealth"* didn't think she should be here and hated everyone and not just me, but for some reason, I had a hard time believing my own theory.

And despite everything, my legs moved toward her. I was drawn to her by my own betraying body, and next thing I knew, I was making another attempt to talk to the brat.

"Should I bring you a blanket? There's one by the couch." I grabbed the rail and leaned forward to take a look at her face. "You seem cold."

Slowly getting out of her daze, she turned to me and locked eyes. It took her a second to realize it was me, and then she furrowed her brows, looking away. "No."

"Are you sure? I can ..."

"Please mind your business. I'm fine." Her voice was sharp, but it trembled. She was cold for sure. The sound of her voice sounded sweet, melodic even, yet she always spoke in such a way that seemed to slice right through my charming smile.

I took a step closer, determined not to be deterred. "Have you ever traveled to the French Riviera before?"

"I have," she answered impatiently.

"I see." Well, that explained how comfortable she looked anywhere, even in this massive villa. "Do you like it?"

She refused to turn her head. "What I would like is to be left alone, please."

There were two things I knew about women. When they wanted to be bothered and when they didn't. Growing up with a sister, I had learned to make the distinction between the two, and that made me popular with women. On a random occasion in my youth, I experimented with how far I could go by pushing my sister Flyn in her worst mood to the point where we both ended up in the hospital with physical bruises.

Ever since then, tact has been a skill I have mastered. If a woman didn't want to be bothered, I walked away. But my better judgment didn't seem to help here in making a rational decision, as the last thing I wanted to do right now was leave Vivi alone.

In fact, it seemed like whatever grudge she held was personal and a little less random. So, I finally dared to ask why. If she mentioned her mother ...

"Have I done anything to make you feel uncomfortable?" I asked.

I waited for an answer that never came. She began tapping her heel nervously on the stone ground.

I decided to change topics and not shoot myself in the foot on my own. "You know, I've heard this place has quite a history. This villa. It's pretty interesting to film here."

Finally, she turned to look at me, her piercing gaze locking onto mine. Her eyes were like pools of ice, revealing nothing. "Do I seem interested in a conversation?"

I couldn't help but feel a pang of annoyance at her haughty tone. Nevertheless, I kept my composure and tried to steer the conversation in a more positive direction. For some reason, I didn't want to give up getting a reaction out of her. I wasn't going to let Vaughn Archer sway me, so I couldn't let one spoiled brat do so either, no matter how stunning she was.

"I suppose the bigger question is why aren't you interested in making a conversation? Are you nervous about filming here with more seasoned actresses?"

Once I said the words, I knew I was being petty and an asshole. I'd never been a dick to women. When I provoked her and she turned toward me with a baffled look, I knew that I was now going to regret it.

My mind searched for the easiest way out of this attempt to provoke her. I took a step closer to the rail and leaned my arms on it. I gripped the rail and looked down at the sea.

"Oh ... um. You don't have to worry, you know." I cleared my throat, trying to sound like this was exactly where I was planning on taking that sentence. "I like your take on the role of my mother. I think you bring a unique depth to the character."

She remained cold. That didn't work. "Oh, you think so, do you? Well, that's charming."

It didn't take a genius to see how pissed off she was now. I tried my best to fix it. "You know, you can always ask me if you have any questions about the character ..."

She didn't even let me finish the sentence. "I prefer to let the script guide me, not idle, meaningless chit-chat. If you believe in your scriptwriters and my acting skills, since you chose me, then please don't make such useless points. If I had any questions, I wouldn't have nailed the audition now, would I?"

And that was the drawing point.

I took a deep breath, choosing my words carefully. "Look, I know we haven't exactly hit it off, and I get the feeling you might not like me, but I believe that our collaboration can be so much more helpful here and you'll get through this easier if we find a way to connect, okay? I want to understand your perspective on this whole thing and why you're angry. If there is any problem, just tell me and we will work it out. Josie and I are here to make this experience comfortable and ..."

There was a flicker of vulnerability in her eyes, a glimpse of something beneath the surface. But just as quickly, it was replaced by a steely resolve.

"I don't need your help," she stated firmly. "I'll do my job, and you do yours. We don't need to talk."

I kept reminding myself I was a professional. "Alright, if that's how you feel. But remember, I'm here to support you, darling." I realized I fumbled at the last part. The endearment I had said as a way to soften my words came all the way around to bite me.

"Here to support me, darling?" She sized me up and took a step back from the rail.

"I mean as the head of this whole filming production."

"Then leave me alone and go flirt with some of the other actresses who are more open to chit-chat in the dark and hearing fascinating stories about the villa."

I blinked twice. Did she know about Coco or not? Which one was it?

"I hate to break it to you, but this is far from flirting. All I was doing was being polite. Don't let the 'darling' fool you. I have little patience for snobby actresses who think they are above everyone."

She finally snapped. "All I asked was to be left alone. Is it so impossible to understand that I don't want to be a part of anyone's bed caravan or be talked to like I am in need of a man to charm my frown away? Then even as I drew my boundary, you judged that I was a snob? I have specifically asked to be left alone a number of times, and then, as if your ego couldn't handle being brushed off, you kept making conversation like I would respond positively to a more charming pestering, patronizing, and prompting."

My mouth parted in shock as I watched her walk back inside without a slight regret of what she'd just hurled at me. The sound of water splashing made me turn around. Vaughn was making flips and jumping into the pool, trying to impress Carrie and Elena.

I walked in the same direction as I was headed before, joining Josie and Giles who were talking with the rest of the film crew.

As I approached them, I could overhear part of the conversation.

George, the stylist, was leading the conversation, and I could tell he was telling them some juicy story.

"Yes, it's true," he told Josie. "Nathan Valetta lives near Marseille with Valesca Astor. They even made it in the French papers. Their marriage is on the rocks due to alleged infidelity, and you know it's serious when even the French mention affairs. I mean, it's part of the culture here."

Everyone laughed, and then George looked up and saw me. The smile was instantly wiped from his face, and he nudged Josie to stop laughing. The conversation suddenly went to a still as they stopped.

I really couldn't deal with any shittier atmospheres. I approached their circle and smiled as well. I put an arm around Josie and laughed to wipe out the tension. I didn't need any more of that on this set as Vivi was already carrying the first prize in that department.

"It's funny, so don't worry about it. And please," I waved it off, "don't even feel awkward about it because of me. Nathan might be my half-brother, but it's not like any of us are close to him. He's made it clear he doesn't like any of us either."

They were still quiet, so with one glance at my face, Giles and Josie laughed and then changed the topic.

* * *

The night was drawing to a close, and with most of the staff hitting the rooms, I headed to the room I used as an office to make sure the schedule and everything else was set for tomorrow.

I was going through some papers when I heard a knock on the side of the door. My eyes locked on the figure entering. Coco shut the door behind her and began unbuttoning the first buttons of her white suit. The curves of her breasts were pushing the suit open, revealing that she wore nothing underneath.

In a second, the suit was down on the ground, and she was bare from the waist up with only a diamond necklace around her neck, flickering in the low lights.

I dropped the papers and rested my palms over the desk. "We're not doing this again."

"I was wondering why you were avoiding me all day."

"Your daughter ..."

"Vivi doesn't have to know anything about this."

So Vivi didn't know? She hated me just because she wanted to hate me. She assumed I was a sleazy bastard and ran with that theory? She pushed me away, she insulted me, and she stayed clear of everyone because that was her personality.

She was not who I assumed she was, and that hurt me more than I was willing to admit. Even without knowing what I did, she drew a line between us.

So Coco was right, after all. Vivi was troublesome and problematic.

"I'm not in the mood." I walked over and picked up Coco's suit from the ground, shoving it back in her hands.

She tossed it aside and then grabbed my chin, bringing her lips closer. "Well, I'm in the mood."

"Leave!" I warned her.

"I'm in the mood for rough fucking, and from what I can see on your face, you need it too." She dropped to her knees in front of me and unbuckled my belt hastily. "You're angry, so take it out on me." She yanked the boxers down and then took my cock in her mouth. The feeling sent pleasure waves throughout my whole body. I could feel my cock getting hard.

I sunk my fingers in her hair, shoving my length deeper inside her throat.

I was frustrated. This whole thing was not my fault in the first place. I wasn't attracted to that brat, I never wanted her, so why was it that I hated how she looked at me and how repulsed she acted?

Coco reached backward, unzipping her dress and pulling it down to her waist. Her thin, manicured hand took my cock again, and this time she ran her tongue all the way down my length to my balls.

I tossed my head back and closed my eyes. She took me in her mouth again and began bobbing her head while rhythmically jerking me off. She added pressure with her lips and then tightened the grip on my cock.

Vivi's face came to mind, her unsmiling mouth and provoking blue eyes.

I pulled away from Coco, and she stared up at me with an intense look in her eyes. "Why did you stop?"

I couldn't do this. "Just go."

There was a glare in her eyes before she controlled her emotions and rose from the ground. She walked over to the desk. "I promised you a rough fucking, didn't I?" She took off the rest of the dress and then bent over the desk, perking her ass up at me, thong slipped aside.

Vivi hated me. Despised me for no reason. I walked to the desk, grabbed a condom from the first drawer, and then walked behind Coco.

Once the condom was on, I grabbed her hips and then thrust my cock into her. Only this time, instead of disgust, I tried to picture Vivi in front of me. Her glare, her body, and her pretty but mean mouth.

I grabbed Coco's hair and began fucking her. She tossed her head back and moaned, adjusting to my cock. "Oh god, yes, fuck me like that."

I surrendered to the ever-familiar feeling of sexual satisfaction. Things picked up at a faster pace.

Then in an instant, the gripping fantasy rushed into my head.

What would Vivi's skin taste like on my tongue? How would my name sound coming from her lips as I dove in and out of her? I could almost picture her parted lips gasping for air.

Reality was gone. All I could think was how much I wanted to wipe out that icy exterior from her face, how I wanted to make her yield to me, wrap her legs around me, and take me in like a good girl. Would she like it slow and steady, or would she be a little freak underneath that cold demeanor? Imagining her riding me sent my blood rushing and my heartbeat going.

The pleasure of the very thought was unlike anything. I'd been with so many women, younger, older, brunettes, blondes, and redheads, each more stunning than the other, all unique in their own way, yet none of them had made me yearn to imagine fucking them while being with another.

I gripped Coco's neck and pinned her rougher on the table. She clenched around me. The room smelled of sex, and all I could hear was her moaning and my own breathing. Yet somehow the setting wasn't right; it didn't feel as good.

For the first and last time, just for the sake of getting it out of my system, I went back to picturing Vivi.

Then it was all easier.

I'd watch her face light up as I peeled her clothes off her. I'd watch her react to my stiff cock pressing against her before slipping just the tip in her, teasing until she begged for the rest of me.

I tried to imagine her short, red, polished nails digging into my back and her mouth on mine, kissing me passionately while pressing me down with her legs wrapped around me. My hands on her thighs as I pulled her back to me with every move.

She gasped, she moaned, she took it in, and then her body trembled as she came.

The orgasm hit me, and my whole body throbbed as I came. I gasped for some air and then released the grip I had on Coco.

I remained silent, not sure how to process imagining fucking her daughter instead of her.

Chapter 7

Vivi

I walked into the kitchen, took a cold sandwich from the plates of breakfast options, and then made my way to the counter, spotting the coffee pot.

After the steaming, dark liquid had made it into my system, I could finally think. My mind had been going back and forth about my decision to keep my guard up and stay out of everyone's way after yesterday's exchange with Tate.

I expected him to yield to the harshness of my tone, get upset, and maybe even insult me, but despite slipping once or twice, he didn't full on attack me no matter how rude I was. I wanted to keep him away from me, so why was I feeling so bad for the way I'd treated him and the way I'd snapped?

Most of the fault was on Coco, who had spent the previous hour trying to get me to socialize, knowing exactly how much I didn't want to be there. She pressured and pressed until I had fumes coming out of my head and agreed to leave the room for the team dinner.

All I wanted was to get on a plane and go back. The very thought of talking to anyone sent my body into an offensive mode, and the person who just happened to get the sharp end of it was Tate.

I had originally made a plan to act when they yelled "action" and then go back to my room when they yelled "cut." Talking to anyone, and especially him, was something I wanted to avoid at all costs.

He was exactly the type of person who could make you so comfortable you spill all your secrets to them, and opening up to anyone here seemed like a bad idea.

But after the way he'd responded yesterday, I was starting to doubt the plan I had so carefully formed in my head.

Why did he have to sound so effortlessly kind despite his looks that pointed to a shameless flirt? Was I wrong about him? Maybe the flicker of attraction I saw in his eyes had nothing to do with the professionalism he portrayed.

I started thinking I should apologize. My words went too far, after all.

And maybe Coco was right. I needed to sympathize with someone who had also lost a father. This movie only showed the lengths Tate went to honor the father he knew despite the poor moral history, and he made the best of it to show both good and bad. The script was proof of that.

I took a bite of the sandwich and leaned on the counter, enjoying the silence. Everyone was still either asleep or outside where their usual gathering was.

The silence didn't last long, however. Vaughn Archer had walked into the kitchen wearing a white, Italian dress shirt and a pair of beige shorts, his hair slicked back with a pair of Ray-Ban sunglasses. He made his way straight toward me.

I had no time to react. In a quick few steps, he leaned his imposing size over me, and I tensed up as he reached toward me.

"Good morning." He winked at me, and then I realized he took the coffee pot behind me, pouring himself coffee in a mug.

I didn't bother answering and took a step away from him. Vaughn Archer was everything a woman might find attractive. He was tall with broad shoulders and a ripped muscular body, straight out of the "most handsome man alive" cover. He was quick with his charms, confident, and shamelessly cocky, which made it harder for any woman to resist for too long. To top that off, his unapologetic nature and bad boy reputation was enough reason for women to get swooped in for a night of reckless adventure. It was obvious after yesterday's showing off. Most women were already swooning.

I got the universal appeal, but I couldn't shake off the internal alarm in my head that this man, no matter the charms, was no good. Unlike Tate, who I had made a conscious decision to hate, my reaction to avoid Vaughn was on pure instinct.

"You okay?" He took a sip of coffee and then wiped both sides of his mouth with his fingers. "I won't bite."

I averted my eyes and focused on finishing my breakfast in silence.

"If we are to have an affair, I'm going to need you to look my way and smile as if you can't wait for me to take you to bed."

My head had never snapped back at someone in disgust so fast. "Excuse me?"

"The role, baby." He brought the mug to his chest and leaned on the counter, crossing his ankles. "We need to show some connection on screen."

I narrowed my eyes. "When they yell 'action,' you'll get your connection. In the meantime, keep comments like that to yourself."

He seemed taken back for a second but was quick to snap back and smile. "I didn't mean to insult you. I'm just trying to make conversation. Lighten up."

I turned my head away, hoping he'd take a hint and leave me alone.

"Are you shy?" He took another step toward me to close the gap. "Hm?"

I placed the coffee and the rest of my sandwich down on the counter and dusted off my hands.

"Did I upset you?" He reached forward, brushing my hair away from my face.

I locked eyes with him, rage threatening to pour out. "Never do that again."

He raised his hand in defeat and laughed. "Was that too forward?"

"I have to go practice my lines. Excuse me." I brushed past him, heading out of the kitchen. Unfortunately for me, Coco seemed to show up at that exact moment.

"Vivi!" she yelled at me.

"It's okay, I pushed her too far." Vaughn laughed.

I brushed past her, but she followed after me and grabbed my elbow. "That was so rude. Don't you understand this behavior will get you fired?"

"Good!"

"No, not good." She clenched her jaw in the way she always did when she tried to contain her anger. "You will go back to apologize to him."

"Why? He is the one who crossed the line shamelessly making a pass at me."

"He is the leading man, for fuck's sake." She lowered her tone so as not to get anyone's attention. "He is making an effort to connect with you for a better performance. Get out of your head and be more professional."

I yanked my arm out of her grip and headed out of the villa. I was confused again. Was I overthinking things? Did I really read into his flirting too much? Maybe he didn't have any bad intentions after all.

I seemed to be wrong about Tate, so who was to say that Vaughn didn't have the same good intentions to just converse?

I pressed a palm to my forehead, trying to fight the upcoming headache.

* * *

The nagging feeling of my inner moral voice didn't go away, so before shooting, I went to Vaughn to apologize.

To my surprise, he was mature and apologized to me as well and even told me not to worry about it. After that, the filming began, and everyone seemed to do a great job. The first day of filming was wrapped up with roaring success. The designated scenes were delivered as imagined, and everyone seemed to be happy with it. Including Tate.

I had gone back and forth wondering if I should apologize to him as well, but every time I made eye contact with him, he turned away as if on instinct. He avoided me on purpose, and that was solely my fault.

I should have been more professional despite deciding to keep to myself. If I wanted to earn myself a reputation as difficult to work with, I certainly managed to achieve that. Soon my name would be plastered next to Vaughn's in the papers as second in line for "baddest" in the business—and not in a good way. I needed to rethink my whole approach.

I didn't want to be here, but I was. Maybe I should find a better way to deal with the situation. A more professional way.

The socializing went on right after dinner, so I decided to find Tate and apologize in hopes of fixing the little left of my reputation I had if I wanted to be a successful actress.

I roamed around the villa trying to find him, but everyone was scattered into little groups outside. I threaded outside and made my way toward the guest house.

Just as I was about to turn and head to the tennis court, I spotted the light turn on and off. I stood there, slightly confused, and then saw Vaughn and Elena inside the guest house, clothes flying everywhere. I scurried off, trying to shake off what I'd seen.

Seemed like my intuition of Vaughn was spot on after all. He wasted no time to get Elena in bed after shooting one scene with her today.

I was almost near the tennis court, passing by the garden, when I heard a muffled voice. I took a gentle step forward, my presence unnoticed, as I watched him from a distance. He stood there, his back turned to me, the moonlight on his tousled, blond hair.

He possessed a certain attractiveness that I had never found in any other man, and I was surprised how little effort it took me to recognize Tate just by the shape of his back.

A jolt of something, something I couldn't quite identify, rushed through me. It was a feeling that was both unfamiliar and unsettling. A sensation that was both exhilarating and disconcerting.

But before I could process it, I heard my name. Tate was talking on the phone, and his voice reached my ears in hushed tones.

"... Vivi, oh her," he said, his voice carrying a hint of frustration. "Oh, don't get me started. She's like an ice princess." He paused and then laughed. "Not an ice queen yet, but she's making her way to that throne. She hates everyone, and she made sure we all know it."

My heart sank at his words, a chill coursing through me as if I had been plunged into icy waters. I couldn't make out the other side of the conversation, but it was clear that Tate was talking about me, and his words stung as if my body had been stung by a thousand needles.

I knew I was to blame for the impression he had of me, but considering his attitude and how calmly he handled me the night before, I didn't think he'd gossip about me to someone.

Suddenly he turned around and locked eyes with me. The flicker of surprise was evident. He didn't expect to get caught, and he didn't know what to say.

I had always prided myself on my composure, and on the control I exerted over my emotions. But standing in the moonlit garden, I felt a vulnerability that I had never experienced before. And instead of facing him, like a coward, I ran off.

Chapter 8

Tate

Regret was there. It kept stabbing at me every time my eyes landed on Vivi. It didn't help that she looked immeasurably stunning in the shadows of the palm trees, the sun rays playing on her face. She stood incredibly still as they put the final touches of makeup on her face before shooting her scene. The blonde wig and the white dress gently playing down to her knees, falling down in an effortless grace, squeezed my heart in a cruel grip.

I had wanted to understand Joel through this movie, and that was one of my leading motives. From this point of view, I slowly and surely did.

I could understand my father's pull toward a gorgeous face. The inability to resist a woman who could turn your whole world around with a flash of a warm smile. The kind that would make you abandon all reason to spend nights in tousled sheets making love to her, feeling her burning body underneath your fingertips.

My throat was parched, and she seemed like the only liquid that could soothe it.

I tried to get myself together, but there it was, vivid as a photograph. Her body under mine in a soft, yellow light, her voice whispering and moaning my name in a pleading tone, and her eyes, which were usually so cold, looking into mine gently as she sweetly begged for me to keep moving inside her.

Fuck. I looked away from her and the scene. This was bad. Especially after I fucked her mother.

I headed toward the rail overlooking the sea to take a breath of fresh air.

I felt guilty about everything. Vivi overhearing me venting to Wade, fucking Coco and imagining Vivi instead. Why was I suddenly thinking of her naked body? Was I that horny that I was tossing all logic out of the window? Did I really want to sleep with someone who could be cold both outside and in bed?

The filming went on, and by the end of the day, my guilt had completely taken over. I took refuge in the guest house to take a second to think. Apologizing seemed to be the right decision here, but I couldn't seem to think of the right way to approach her.

"Why are you being antisocial? That's unlike you." Coco walked into the guest house after I disappeared for five minutes. I guess she came to check if I was with someone.

"I'm clearing my head."

"What's on your mind, baby?"

I flinched at the word *baby*. "I might have said something about your daughter over the phone, and she overheard me."

"What did you say?"

"I called her an ice princess."

I didn't expect Coco to burst out laughing. She tossed her head back and ran a finger under her eye. "Oh, that's a good one."

"You're not angry?"

"She's exactly like that, why would I be?" She approached me, but I rose from the couch and walked farther away from her.

"Don't you think I should apologize to her?" I asked.

"I mean, she was eavesdropping, right?"

I raised a brow. "I think it was more accidental."

She sighed. "Don't let it bother you. She's always been like that. Always plays the victim. It's been her narrative for two years now. Vivi channels any annoyances into her performance, so her being insulted makes her a better actress. Trust me, you've done her a favor. It's not like she's not aware of what people think of her and her attitude. I keep telling her to fix it, but she's headstrong like that. I'm here to make sure she doesn't get out of control."

I was a little taken aback by how nonchalant Coco seemed. And unmotherly. It might have been due to my own subjective view on mothers, considering mine would have done anything for us and would crush any insult thrown our way. Wade, Flyn, and I weren't exactly exemplary children, yet she never let anyone say anything bad about us. So was this how other mothers acted? Was I overthinking this? Or did Coco care less about her daughter than I thought?

Coco didn't let that brew long in my head. She walked over to me and tried to reach my belt. I took her hand off without a word and then left the guest house.

Chapter 9

Vivi

A week had passed since we started filming, and the tension between Tate and I wasn't going away. He seemed even colder than usual, and I refused to spare him more than a second glance. Acting came as breathing to me, but I wasn't going to spare even an inch of that talent to appease someone so quick to judge.

It hurt me more than I expected that he thought of me as some snob who looked down on people when he didn't even have the slightest idea of what it was like to be me. To be in my shoes. No amount of money could buy you happiness or bring someone back from the dead. Most people with money knew that. I couldn't snap out of it like my father never existed, and that was all anyone seemed to want me to do. Coco pushed and pushed and pushed until I was filled with so much anger and revolt that I couldn't control who got hit with it.

And that seemed to make me the worst person to be around during filming. No matter how he saw me, it was too late to fix it now, so I decided to just ride it out.

During our break, I sat down by the pool. The sun was more blinding than usual, so I fixed the hat on my head and narrowed my eyes to make out the silhouette approaching me.

"Getting a tan?" Vaughn Archer sat down on one of the pool chairs next to me. "Or warming your cold heart?" A friendly grin spread across his face.

Instead of taking it to heart as I would usually do, I smiled. While the past week seemed like everyone hated me, with Tate being on top of that list, Vaughn Archer changed his tune from day one. He was kinder, friendlier, and even gentler to me after I apologized.

I was still on the fence, but having someone not shooting glares at me was helpful. He made the occasional jokes to make me laugh but never crossed the line with me again.

"I'm trying to get some peace and quiet before I go back to shooting for the next scene. Aren't you dying in that?" I took a look at his outfit. He wore ripped and stone-washed denim and an oddly striped t-shirt with a jacket on top to add to Joel's style in the 80s. But in this heat, he must have been dying.

"I got used to wearing suits in LA in the broad daylight. This is nothing." His smile was convincing. "You have it better off though in that blue button-up dress."

"I have to thank Marianne for that." I gripped my hat and tossed my head back with a smile. "She seemed to love this style and wasn't that fond of heat."

Vaughn stared at me a little bit longer than usual. "You know, when you're not frowning, you have a very nice smile. It's nice to see it once in a while."

Vaughn could be a nice guy if he wanted to. His words might have even been honest. But my instincts never let me drop my guard. I smiled politely and changed the topic. "How are things going with Elena? I don't see you sneaking out every break."

He shrugged and let out a long, tired sigh. "Ah, she broke my heart. The fun was over before it even began. I guess that's what I get for messing around with someone who is playing a mistress."

The comment didn't sit right with me, but saying something about it might have turned the last person here against me.

"Come on." He got up and extended his hand.

"Where?" I asked.

"Let's take a walk around the premises of the villa. We only have about twenty minutes left, and we can use the change of scenery."

We had twenty minutes and nothing better to do, so I took his hand, and he helped me up. "Okay, lead the way."

Vaughn and I took the stone pathway around the villa, promenading under the shades of the trees, looking at some of the other villas peeking over the fences. He told me stories about his earliest acting days without probing any of mine, and I could enjoy the soft breeze on my face without trying to put up a front.

By the time we got back, I already felt better and gave one of the best scenes I had delivered so far.

Tate

So, the ice princess could smile after all, just not for me.

While walking from one set to another, I spotted Vivi by the pool talking to none other than Vaughn fucking Archer.

She seemed to smile at something he said, tossing her head back and looking up at him with warmth she refused to show me.

Anger and jealousy took over without any reason. She was just another empty-headed girl who fell recklessly for the charms of some idiot who knew exactly what to say and how to act to get her to respond to him.

He was a talented actor and even more talented at reading people. Was Vivi so stupid to let herself get swayed by a few nice words and insincere politeness?

At least I was honest with her.

A glimpse of my first attempt to sway her popped into my head, and I remembered how disastrous it was. It took an even bigger swing at my ego. Okay, maybe I did try to sway her with those intentions at the beginning as well.

But why did I care if she liked Vaughn better than me?

Just because I fucked her in my head a few times didn't mean I had feelings for her.

He suddenly gave her his hand, and she took it. As she rose to her feet, he steadied her to the ground and let his lingering eyes stay on her face for a few moments before releasing her.

His intentions were so fucking obvious, and she was going with it? Where was the ice princess now? Couldn't she hurl the same insults at him?

I clenched my fists, my knuckles turning white as I fought to control the resentment bubbling up within me. Why him? Why not me?

Jealousy gnawed at me without explanation, leaving a bitter taste in my mouth. What did he have that I didn't? Was I not worthy of her kindness?

Vivi

After filming was over and we waited for dinner, I sat alone outside on one of the couches in the summer kitchen. I could hear crickets somewhere in the back, the perfect backdrop for a summer evening.

I saw Coco make her way across the pool, walking toward me. She seemed more discontented than usual.

"Well, seems like you've done it now." She handed me a tablet and pointed at the screen. "You look like a lovely couple."

My breath never left my lungs.

I scrolled through the paparazzi pictures on the tablet, my heart pounding in my chest as I stared at the images of Vaughn and me. The headlines screamed "Hottest New Couple?" in bold, attention-grabbing letters. My blood ran cold as I saw the way the photographers had captured our moment together by the pool.

In one of the photos, Vaughn was helping me out of a pool chair, his hand gently holding mine, but what was a meaningless, innocent gesture and just a simple act of kindness was spun into something entirely different.

I clenched my teeth together, frustration and anxiety welling up inside me. The pictures were misleading, taken out of context to create a narrative that simply wasn't true. Vaughn and I were not a couple and were never going to be romantically involved.

As I continued to scroll through the images, I saw captions speculating about our "secret romance" and "steamy rendezvous between filming breaks." The comments from fans and gossip-hungry followers were a mix of excitement and curiosity, all assuming there was something more between us. I could already feel the weight of the rumors, the invasion of my privacy.

"I guess you're not used to the scandals yet." Coco sighed. "Well, it works in your favor, baby. It will stir up the perfect publicity."

My fingers trembled as I thought about how this would affect both Vaughn and me. Our careers were on the line here, and the last thing we needed was the distraction of false romance rumors.

"Can't we address this and deny it?" I asked.

Coco seemed insulted by the idea. "Darling, this is free publicity. If we comment on this, people will suspect even more. Where there is smoke, there are flames."

I pushed my hair back and kept scrolling back and forth between pictures. "I just don't understand how the press could have gotten photos from inside the grounds."

The more I looked at them, the more staged they felt, like they were taken from the inside by someone in the villa. Vaughn seemed to stand in perfect pose for the shot. Doubts began to creep into my mind.

"I think they used telephoto lenses," Coco said, but the more I looked, the more certain I was that this was staged by someone.

I was so distracted that I didn't notice someone had stood behind me until they extended their hand and grabbed the tablet from me.

I turned around to see Tate looking at the pictures and headlines. His closeness sent my heart racing.

As he leaned on the headrest on the couch, I could hear his breathing. There was a subtle scent of cologne mingled with the faint aroma of coffee from earlier. In the soft light by the pool and the close proximity, I could see the details on his face like the light dusting of stubble on his strong jaw, his soft, captivating, blue eyes veiled behind long, dark lashes.

He stared at the picture on the tablet, and the silence stretched. His body tensed up before he forced a smile on his face.

His eyes, however, stared at me in a cold glare. "Are congratulations in order?"

"It's fake news," I replied, feeling my throat going dry. Did he really believe that? For some reason, I didn't want Tate to think I was another girl who would fall for Vaughn Archer.

"You seem pretty cozy together," he pressed on.

I swallowed the heaviness of his words. "He was being nice to me."

"That very nice gesture seemed to work. You gave your best performance after this, didn't you?"

That was true, but only because after a week of torture and Coco's endless scrutiny, I could finally relax. The more I tried to explain myself to him, the worse it felt. "It wasn't because of him."

"Don't be shy if you like him, darling," Coco intervened. "I heard he's a great lover."

I could see Tate's jaw clench. "I don't mind if you're fucking him either. A little whoring around is all part of the fun on movie sets, don't you think?" His voice was cold and biting as he said it.

The shock of his words was like a bucket of cold water poured over me. I felt the heat rise to my cheeks, and tears welled up in my eyes. "I'm not a whore."

I got up and pushed past him, running back into the house. I could hear Coco tossing a remark about another one of my "emotional outbursts" followed by a burst of laughter. God forbid she lost face because of me.

The tears started to fall, betraying my hurt and confusion. I had never imagined he would react this way.

I could see Vaughn heading outside the house and a smile curving on his face. "Hey."

I remembered the photos and how perfectly posed he was in them. Who was to say he didn't orchestrate it on his own for some more drama and publicity? It was what he did best, after all, and he used me for it.

I pushed past him and ran to my room.

Tears streamed down my face. Tate wasn't anyone important. I didn't care about him. So why was I so hurt by being accused so cruelly of something so hurtful, something that wasn't true at all?

Tate

I watched her rush off in tears, and my chest clenched in pain. I couldn't tear my eyes off her back until she was gone from my sight.

"Did that bother you?" Coco's cold voice broke the silence.

I turned to her, hands shoved in the pockets of my shorts, and smiled. "No, why would it?"

She tilted her head, observing me, and then picked up the tablet I had tossed on the couch and stared at the pictures.

"Well, if you say so, then it must be true." She turned the tablet toward me again. "But take a good look. Does this look like the face of someone unbothered?"

In the very photos, I could see myself in the back, glaring at Vaughn this afternoon as I saw him being intimate with Vivi. The jealousy was framed on my face in the most obvious way.

"That's me squinting. The sun was pretty rough today." I smiled, relaxing my shoulders.

"If you don't care then," she placed the laptop down and wrapped her arms around my shoulders, "why don't we continue our thing somewhere private?"

I removed her hands. "That and this has nothing to do with each other."

I walked back into the house, feeling the imposing weight of my actions again. If Vivi did sleep with Vaughn, would she have reacted the way she did? Things were making less and less sense every day.

Chapter 10

Tate

I waited by the villa's open, heavy, iron entrance gates as the black BMW convertible drove in and parked in the open cobblestone space. She moved the dark-shaded glasses from her eyes to the top of her head and got out of the car wearing a white, Chanel, plaid crop top and skirt while heavy, gold earrings hung from her ears.

"You just had to go all out, didn't you?" I walked over to her.

"I like arriving in style." Flyn tossed her hands around my neck, swooping me in for a hug. I instinctively reached for her hair bun, which seemed professionally styled. Her usual messy hairstyle was gone.

"Touch my hair and you're dead," she threatened immediately.

I laughed. "All dolled up, who are you trying to impress?"

She pulled away from the hug to take a look at me. She squinted as the noon sun was up and heavy in her eyes.

"You're here to work, I'm here on vacation. Might as well enjoy some attention." She sized me up. "You, on the other hand, seem tired. Everything okay with shooting?"

"Yeah, just a lot of work. Come, I'll introduce you to the cast and crew." I swiftly changed the topic as I didn't feel like explaining that the lack of sleep was mainly because of Vivi and our argument yesterday.

"Please. Let's get out of this sun and get a virgin mojito." She took the lead, walking ahead.

"That's about the only virgin you can get around here," I muttered behind her.

Vaughn and Carrie were practicing their lines in the shade by the pool. They both stood as they saw us approaching. Vaughn was the first to extend his hand to greet my sister.

"Vaughn." The grin on his face lingered. Unbelievable. Elena, Vivi, and now my sister? If he was involved with Vivi, how dare he try to flirt with my sister? The anger was lit up in me again, but I tried to shove it down with a professional smile.

"Flyn." She shook his hand and then turned to Carrie. "Hi, I'm Flyn, nice to meet you."

"I'm Carrie." Carrie shook my sister's hand and turned to me. "You two look nothing alike."

"I got the good looks in the family." Flyn grinned. "He just got whatever was left."

"Decency, common sense?" I teased.

"Certainly a sense of humor," she retorted.

Carried laughed. "Oh, I wish I had a sibling. You guys seem very close. It's nice to have you here." She glanced at Flyn and paused before completely breaking into a grin. "I'm sorry, you must hear this often, but you are even more gorgeous in person."

"And taller." Flyn shrugged, but a content smile spread on her face. "And you're even nicer than I've heard. How about we girls grab ourselves a nice drink, and you can tell me how the shooting is going so far?"

Vaughn's eyes followed my sister as she made her way to the summer kitchen's bar.

I crossed my arms over my chest. "Is any woman safe around you?"

"Jealous, old man?" Vaughn smiled and picked up his script from the pool chair.

"I'd be more careful if I was you. Your career depends on this movie, and I don't think your reputation can take any more damage. One wrong step, and I won't hesitate to remove you from the role if you do anything to ruin my movie."

"Is that a threat?" He glared at me.

"It's a warning." My tone carried an edge, and I could taste the tension in the air.

A vein popped on the side of Vaughn's forehead, but he decided to back down, and without a word, he left.

* * *

Somewhere around lunch break, Flyn and I went for a touristy spin of the place, then sat down at one of the restaurants with a view of the sea. One of the passions we both shared was food. From lobster, lean fish, oysters to shrimp salad, we tasted it all.

"I am stuffed." Flyn rummaged in her bag, taking out her packs of cigarettes. She took one out and lit it up, then took a hit. She then took a whiff of the salty air of the sea and relaxed in her seat. "Europeans know good food and how to enjoy life."

"And we still haven't had desert."

"I'm glad you got me to come here. New York was beginning to be boring."

I shrugged. "That's a roundabout way of telling me you miss me. What? Wade was not as much fun as me?"

She chuckled. "Oh, don't get me started. If I had to hear one more thing about his sappy love life, I was going to drown myself in the Hudson."

"He did become practically impossible after getting married. He keeps tossing his happy life in my face."

"What does he know? Does he enjoy a good lobster and a smoke at the French Riviera? I don't think so."

Both Flyn and I gave each other a look and then smiled. It wasn't the same without him with us. He might not have the same passion for food as we had, but we still preferred a trio over a duo.

Flyn raised her hand, ordering dessert in French, and tossed a flirty smile at the waiter.

"Now you use French, couldn't you have said something when I was ordering lunch?"

"What and miss watching you struggle your way through the menu? What do you take me for?"

"I always forget Mom taught you French when you started your modeling career."

"Hey, if it's anything French, I'm good at it." She took a final hit of the cigarette and then put it out in the ashtray. "So, how about you tell me now why the long face? You think I can't tell when something is bothering you? Unlike Wade, you don't have a poker face."

I really didn't want to get too much into it, but now that she brought it up ...

"I'm having problems with one of the actresses."

"Who?" Flyn leaned forward, curious to see if I was going to let her in on some interesting rumor.

"Vivi Astor. The woman is infuriating," I blurted out, but her face and tears from yesterday ran through my mind. It was gnawing away at me. "She is cold and obnoxious."

"Ah, she got you using big words."

"Refuses to play nice with everyone," I continued. "Thinks she is better than everyone, so she ignores any polite conversation anyone starts with her." I paused. "Well, almost everyone."

"I see."

"I mean, how can she be so good on camera and so irritating off it? One moment she captivates everyone, and we are happy with how the scene turned out, so I try to talk to her, and the next minute she snarls like a vicious cat. It's exhausting trying to keep up with her. She is driving me insane."

Flyn blinked. "Wow, this is the first time I've seen you be this mad at a woman. You've always worked your way around them even if they found some way to reject you."

"I can't get through to her. She is impossible."

"No wonder you look like that. Must be hard, particularly since you like her."

"Me? Like her?" I snorted. Was I that obvious? "I think she is beautiful, but beyond that ..."

Flyn nodded, completely entertained. "I meant as an actress."

I ran a hand through my hair. "I don't get it. She gets upset every time she hears something about herself she doesn't like, yet is completely aware she earned that reputation on her own."

"What did you say?"

"I might have called her an ice princess while I was talking to Wade, and she overheard me. But It's not like I wasn't right. And yesterday ..."

"What happened yesterday?" Flyn took out another cigarette.

"There were photos that came out with her and Vaughn taking a walk around the villa. The man is on a mission to fuck every woman in the house, and the innocent pictures were practically nothing, but she was so upset by it. I might have told her that whoring around the movie set is part of the fun, but she took it so personally and ran out in tears."

"You made her cry because you were jealous?"

"I ... I wasn't jealous ..." Fuck, I made her cry because I was jealous.

Flyn covered her face with one hand, trying to hold back laughter. "Tate."

"Okay, maybe I was jealous, but not because they're fucking, but because she showed she can actually be nice to someone, so why can't she show the same fucking decency and respect toward everyone else in the house?"

Flyn wiped a tear from her eye from laughing. "I never took her for the type to get under men's skin like this."

"Wait until you meet her."

"Oh, I know her alright, but what you're telling me is a bit hard to believe."

I raised a brow. "Did you meet her at one of your fashion shows or something?"

Flyn lit up her next cigarette. "No, at rehab."

For the first time today, I could hear myself think loud and clear. "Vivi was in rehab for drugs?" Somehow even I had a hard time believing it.

Flyn shook her head in denial. "In the facility I was staying at, there were many different departments. My shrink thought it might be good for me to talk to someone who was also dealing with the loss of someone close to them as I was. It was around the time Mom died, so she took me to Vivi's department. The suicide attempt patients."

My blood ran cold as I heard that.

Flyn went on. "I was out for a smoke, I saw her next to me, and started a conversation. But the girl I met and the one you're describing sound like two absolutely different people. I got a completely different impression."

I couldn't say anything, so I waited for her to carry on.

"She was in there after her father's death. She was very close to him before he died so it hit her hard. It was nice to talk to someone who actually had a good father. She told me stories about him, and I told her about mom. Though I don't think she knew at that point that Marianne Blanchard was my mother. Maybe my stories impacted her subconsciously and that's why she has such a good grasp of mom's character. Either way, we became good friends there, and we still keep in touch."

"Why didn't you say anything when I told you her name?"

"I didn't want to influence your choice just because I knew her. I thought she'd tell you when you started shooting and get to know each other, but this was a surprise. I never expected this."

"That she'd hate me this much?"

"I doubt she hates you. She is this sweet, innocent girl who was sheltered from all the bad things in the world."

"Meanwhile she's fucking around with Vaughn Archer."

Flyn put out her cigarette and took a sip from the water. "Vaughn? Please. It's so far-fetched. She's too smart to go for him. Not to mention I think she's still ... well, you know."

I waited, but she didn't finish the sentence. "What?"

"A virgin," Flyn blurted out. "I can ask her about it, but even if she isn't, 'whoring around' is way off the mark. That's why she got upset."

If that was the truth, I had fucked up big time and was overdue for some apologies.

* * *

The final scene of shooting for today was finally wrapped up. Most of the cast and crew was already making dinner plans when I saw Vivi quietly step away and head into the kitchen.

I excused myself and walked over to the entrance of the kitchen. I saw her taking some fruit snacks, and then she turned to leave.

"Making a grab and running for it?" I smiled.

She plastered the same cold look on her face she liked scaring people off with. She tried to ignore me and pass by, but I moved in the same direction she did, and she eventually had to stop and look at me properly.

"Move!" She looked up at me, and even though she was seething, there was something inexplicably adorable about the way her eyes narrowed, a mean look that clashed with her tiny, delicate features.

I took a step closer, and the height difference between us was stark. I couldn't help but notice how petite she seemed, almost fragile in contrast to my frame. She barely reached my chest, and in that moment, I felt an overwhelming need to protect her, even though the source of her distress was me.

Her lips formed a tight line. The wooden floor creaked beneath my feet as I edged closer.

The scent of her shampoo lingered under my nose mixed with the remnants of half-peeled tangerines on the kitchen counter, a mess from her attempt to make a snack.

My gaze lingered on her, taking in the subtle details that made her irresistible. The soft curve of her cheek, flushed in anger, the strands of hair that had escaped her tiny bun, and the way her lashes fluttered in annoyance. Every detail only added to her allure, and it made my chest ache with longing.

"Let's talk."

She averted her eyes, her gaze fixed on the floor, but I could sense the wariness in her posture softening.

I longed to bridge the distance between us, to reach out and touch her. As I raised my hand toward her shoulder, she winced. "We have nothing to talk about."

"Yes, we do." I took a step forward, and she instantly took a step back.

"Are you going to toss more insulting words my way?" she asked.

"Are you going to keep glaring?" Hearing from Flyn what she was really like, it was a lot easier to take her anger. "Come on, five minutes."

"No." She gritted her teeth.

I relaxed my shoulders. "Give me a chance to apologize and make things right."

"To apologize?" Her cold, defensive exterior seemed to vanish, and I could see those vulnerable deer eyes she only showed on camera.

Flyn was right. This was the real Vivi. Once I could see past her defenses, it was easy to see how innocent she was and how desperate she was to hide that part of herself.

"Yes, I want to apologize for what I said yesterday and for calling you an ice princess. I was venting to my brother, but it was never meant to be thrown at you. You and I might have had our differences, but I still don't think it was right of me to act that way and say that."

She was trying to come up with something to throw back, only to just give up and lower her head.

"I'm sorry as well. I was going to apologize, but then it seemed like you were ignoring me, so I didn't try too hard to change your mind about me." She finally glanced up with gleaming puppy eyes. "Is it too late to call a truce?"

I couldn't believe it. She was so sweet, and I didn't know what took me aback more. The fact that she apologized as well or that another strong tug of desire pulled at me.

"Truce sounds good to me." The happy smile curved on my face without even trying.

Vivi smiled shyly, and then she slid past me, heading back to her room. I stood there grinning like an idiot for a few seconds before I realized what I was doing.

Now that the hostilities were out of the way, I could finally admit to myself how much I liked her.

* * *

I was passing through the hallways on my way to Flyn's room when I heard the piano coming from downstairs.

The soft strains of a familiar melody drifted through the air, caressing my ears like a gentle breeze. It was a tune I hadn't heard in years. My heart skipped a beat as the notes resonated. They carried a certain warmth I hadn't felt in a long time.

It was my mother's favorite song to hum in the mornings and before bed when she was putting us to sleep.

I paused in my tracks, my hand gripping the handrail. Before I knew it, I was heading downstairs.

The room was bathed in soft lamplight, and Vivi sat at the piano, her fingers gliding effortlessly over the keys. She was lost in the music, her eyes closed, her expression one of pure concentration. I hovered over the rail, unsure if I should approach her.

It felt like an intrusion, like I was eavesdropping on something deeply private. But the pull was irresistible.

I didn't know how long I stood there, lost in the music and the sight. When Vivi finally finished playing, she opened her eyes and turned to see me standing by the stairs. She looked surprised but not alarmed.

"I'm sorry. I really didn't mean to pry while you're playing," I said.

"That's alright." She pulled the sleeves of her cardigan down nervously. "I didn't realize I had an audience."

I cleared my throat as I replied, "That was beautiful. It was my mother's favorite song."

A sympathetic smile played on Vivi's lips. "My father's too." She patted the space beside her on the piano bench. "Come sit down," she invited me.

I hesitated before accepting her offer, unsure how she'd view it, but I walked over nevertheless and took a seat beside her.

Vivi's voice was warm and comforting. "I didn't know it was your mother's favorite. I played it because it reminds me of my father. He used to play it with me all the time." She pressed her fingers over the keys, playing the beginning again.

"He taught you how to play?" I asked.

"Yes, because he wanted to torment me." She smiled, but her eyes gleamed in sadness. "It's called 'La Boheme,' an older French ballad. My father would come down for breakfast and sing it to me every morning. It made me laugh, but I begged him to stop. So, he moved on to playing it on the piano. I never knew there would be a time when I would miss his loud voice in the morning."

She blinked away her tears and smiled at me. "Your mother had good taste in music."

I reached forward and wiped the tear under her eye. "We never know how short time is with someone until they're gone."

She sighed. "Do you miss your mother?"

"Every day." I nodded, struggling to find the words to express what I was feeling. "But it's like she was here with me for just a moment. Thank you."

Vivi smiled gently. "I know I was being harsh the first time, but I hope I'm doing your mother justice with this role."

I looked down at the piano and pressed a few random keys. "She'd be pleased in every way that you're playing her. You are extraordinary."

The room seemed to fill with silence. I glanced at her to see her staring at me with tenderness, cheerfulness, and at ease. How the hell did I ever mistake her for someone cold and unaffectionate? The reality was staring me in the face, but I clouded my judgment with pointless pride.

"I'm going to bed." Vivi slid off the piano bench, and there was an embarrassed flush on her face. "I'm glad we worked everything out. Have a good night."

"Goodnight." I smiled and watched her rush upstairs.

I stared into nothing for a little while, alone with my thoughts, before I heard heels clinking on the upstairs floor, and a minute later Coco came downstairs.

She stared at me with a vicious glare I hadn't seen before.

"I'm not in the mood for whatever fight you are trying to pick." I tried to pass her, but she grabbed my elbow.

"I'm not one of your little girls that you can fuck whenever you like and then just dismiss me."

"You have this all wrong ..." I took her hand down. "Sleeping together was a mistake in the first place."

The words hung in the air, and there was silence as Coco processed what I had just said. Then, her expression shifted from one of surprise to disbelief, and finally, to anger.

"What the hell are you talking about?" she spat out. Her voice was sharp and accusatory. "You wanted me."

I had nothing to say. If anything, I wanted Vivi. It was always Vivi from day one.

She scoffed, her eyes narrowing in anger. Her frustration was evident. Her eyes were filled with resentment. "You're just a selfish prick who can't handle commitment. Maybe working as a porn star would do that to a person."

I didn't respond to that either. It was best to just let her vent.

"Are you fucking someone else?"

"No."

The silence lingered, and she stormed back upstairs.

Chapter 11

Vivi

Coco was gone all morning. I don't know what prompted her to just disappear, but for some reason, the tension seemed to leave my body, and I could finally relax. Most of the cast and crew had gone to film at another location, so I had the villa to myself.

I roamed around the premises when I saw a shadow moving into the guest house. I approached the window to see Tate on the phone with someone. He was holding up papers, rummaging through them while holding the phone between his shoulder and chin, so I figured it was an important call.

I was going to leave him to it when he spotted me, and a boyish grin spread across his face. He took the phone in his hand and then waved at me.

I raised my arms and waved back. Heat rushed to my face. Why was I suddenly so self-aware?

He prompted me to come inside the house. I took a turn from the cobblestones and walked over to the door of the guest house.

I reached for the door, but he opened it before me and waved me inside while still talking on the phone.

"Yes, yes. Uh-uh ..." Tate held the door still open while he talked. "Alright, I will relay that to Director Giles. Alright. We will continue this later, thank you for calling outside your work time. I appreciate it."

He hung up and smiled at me again. "Hi."

"Hey." I smiled back. "I was just passing through, didn't want to bother you."

"I am almost done." He walked over to the window couch, gathering the papers on it into one messy pile. "I was going to head out for lunch, want to join me?"

"Isn't your sister joining you?"

He shook his head as he rushed from one end of the room to another, picking up his stuff, then stopped by the coffee table, finishing his coffee. "Flyn took off with Carrie, who offered to keep her company on a tour of the city while the rest were shooting. I was going to eat alone, so you keeping me company works out great."

Before I could argue, he pressed a hand on my back and nudged me outside of the guest house.

An hour later, we were sitting in a nearby restaurant finishing a nice meal, and I was surprised at how funny Tate was.

At first glance, he looked like a guy who never took anything seriously, then after working with him, I thought he was a selfish asshole who wanted to poke fun and hit on me, but the man before me was neither.

He was effortlessly charming, sweet, dedicated, and passionate. He had a whirlwind of stories to share, ways to make someone laugh and make them feel comfortable even without having an agenda.

We talked about our passion for food and hobbies and spun many other topics before we somehow made our way around back to work.

"I'm telling you it is traumatic seeing Vaughn play Joel, especially with you as Marianne."

"Why?" I brought the glass to my lips, finishing my drink.

"Because you play it so well." He laughed. "I think part of me wants to see it, and part of me hates it because I never had it."

"A father?" I asked, unsure how much he wanted to talk about the topic.

"We had a father, more or less." Tate called for the check and reached for his drink. "Flyn, Wade, and I grew up thinking Slade was our father. Not that he was around much. He drank, gambled, and tried out every vice you could think of. As if ignoring his kids wasn't enough, he didn't help out Mom in any way. I have no idea why she ever made us call him 'dad' when he was never one. And hadn't been one till the end. Wouldn't even come to see her while she battled cancer."

"I'm sorry ..." I reached forward and touched his hand. "But she had you three."

"Yes, but would it not have been better to have someone by her side who could help her too? Who could help all of us? Joel might not have been the most honorable person, but I think he was a good father. Watching you and Vaughn play my parents makes me think of how different life would be for me if he had been in our lives growing up."

"I heard you're close to your half-brother. How does he feel about all of this?"

"He has his own take on it. His life wasn't perfect either, but when Joel decided he wanted to take the world by the horns, he took Ethan with him. They stuck together and made history."

I nodded, unsure what to say.

"Enough about me. Tell me about your father."

"Ah, well, I don't know if there is so much to talk about."

"Start somewhere; I'm curious. Just a moment though."

Tate picked up the check, and we headed back to the villa on foot.

"My dad was my hero. There was nothing he wouldn't do to protect me, and growing up with him was fun."

Tate and I took slow steps back to the villa, shoulder to shoulder, as if coming back home from a date. The very thought of it was nerve-wracking.

"I loved doing things with him. We'd go traveling and do hobbies together. He was just full of life. As I got older, we didn't hang around as much, but he was still my biggest supporter. He encouraged me to give acting a try."

Tate listened carefully without interrupting.

"Then the tragedy happened, and well, I'm sure you know the rest. Flyn must have told you."

"She told me how you met," Tate confirmed. "As someone who has lost both parents, trust me, I understand your pain more than anything."

I smiled. "Thank you. That's comforting to hear."

We walked in silence, and I kept glancing at him from the corner of my eye.

Tate slowed his steps, and I followed suit until we both came to a halt in front of the villa.

His eyes locked onto mine and sent shivers down my spine. There was an unspoken chemistry in the air, and I was feeling it. Heavy and electric. I held my breath, bracing myself for what was to come.

There was a brief second of hesitation as if he were searching for the perfect way to phrase it, and then he just sighed. "I know this isn't any of my business, but is there something going on with you and Vaughn, or was that picture completely taken out of context?"

My heart pounded in my chest. Was he asking as a producer, or was he asking as a man who was jealous?

I was about to answer when there was a loud shrieking on the streets as a fast car with tinted windows parked in front of the villa. Coco came out of the passenger seat, and the car drove off just as fast.

"What are the both of you doing outside?" She suspiciously glanced at both of us.

"We went out for lunch," Tate answered.

"Oh really?" She turned toward me, raising a brow. I just knew she had something to say about this.

"I'm going back to my room. I think the sun got to me. Excuse me." I rushed inside, and I could hear Coco's heels click on the path behind us. I hurried my steps inside, but Coco followed right behind me. She was not going to let me off the hook.

"Playing around with Tate now, are we? Vaughn wasn't enough of a toy?"

I sighed. "I wasn't playing. We just went for lunch."

"Didn't I give you a strict meal plan to follow? And instead of running around town, it wouldn't kill you to put on a mask or so; you look so blotchy."

There it was—the nagging. The constant patronizing and voice of insane reason in my head.

"Fine, can I have a nap now? I have a headache."

I closed the door on her and then tossed myself on the bed. For the first time, her words didn't sting that much, and I was in a good mood. I was going to be out of her grip the moment I turned twenty-one, and with the way I felt after having lunch with Tate, I had a feeling the days to my birthday were going to pass much sooner.

* * *

I sat in the shade by the pool going over my lines. My scenes were next, but considering how long they were taking to shoot the scene on the tennis court, it was going to take a while. Flynn, who was playing around in the summer kitchen for a while, came out carrying two cold lemonades with cute umbrellas in the glasses.

"For you." She handed me one.

"Thank you. I needed this." I took a sip of the cold beverage and placed it next to my script.

"They sure are taking long." Flyn lay down on the couch and put her feet up on the coffee table. Her model legs went on for days, every part of her skin looked like perfection, and even without makeup, up her skin was glowing.

"You look much better these days," I blurted out without thinking.

"Thanks." She lowered her shades down to her nose. "Wade and Tate have been doting on me ever since I got out of rehab."

"I'm glad to hear you guys are even closer."

"We are. Wade recently got married."

"I heard."

"Well, not as much as I have." Flyn chuckled and then sighed as if the very topic tired her. "He was such a keep it to yourself guy, then overnight he became such a chatterbox over how happy he is being married and how we should settle down. And we are happy for him, but Tate and I started feeling like we're at those weddings where distant relatives you barely talk to keep asking you when you are going to settle down and get married."

I laughed. "Well, are you seeing anyone?"

She paused. "No."

"Ah, but there is someone." I took a sip of the lemonade.

"There is someone I have my eye on." She smiled. "What about you? What is this about Vaughn Archer I heard? Are the papers right for once?"

"No, god no." I shook my head. "Vaughn is not even my type."

"I see. I figured he is not your cup of tea."

"I'm just not into guys like that. Rugged troublemakers are not really my thing."

Flyn raised her shades and glanced at me while playing with the little umbrella in her glass. "Well, what is your type?"

"I like someone who is funny and good with people. Someone who can make everyone comfortable around them. Someone passionate and hungry for life, yet incredibly devoted when they find something or someone they like. Someone sweet despite having it rough in life." I pushed my hair back as my thoughts formed Tate's image in my head.

"I see." Flyn glanced at me and smirked before focusing back on her lemonade. She didn't say anything, but we both knew what that entertained smile meant.

Chapter 12

Tate

"Vaughn, Vaughn! Focus!" Giles yelled. "You keep walking out of frame."

For some reason, Vaughn was off his game today, and it had cost us half a day of redoing scenes over and over again. At this point, Giles was getting agitated, Vaughn was sweating in the sun, losing patience, and about to snap, and the cast was walking on a tightrope, unsure what to do about it.

"Alright, everyone." I clapped my hands. "How about we take a break, have some cooling drinks by the bar, and go back to work in about twenty minutes?"

"But ..." Giles was about to argue, but I walked over to him. "I know you want to finish the scene. Give me a chance to talk to Vaughn. I'll get him in shape, and you'll have your scene today. But I need to see what's going on."

Giles was too tired to argue. He sighed and then waved me off.

I grabbed one of the ice bottles of water and walked over to Vaughn, pushing him into the shade. I handed him the bottle.

"What's the problem, Vaughn? You were killing these scenes until yesterday."

He chugged down his water and then sat down. Exhausted, stressed, and ready to quit, Vaughn seemed to need venting.

He extended his hand as he was about to explain something and glanced up at me. "Man to man here. I've been working my ass off at wooing her, yet she keeps drawing a straight line with me and is pissing me off. I'm horny, and I want her, and she just won't give in."

"Wait, hold on. Who are we talking about here? Elena?"

"Vivi." He snapped his fingers, annoyed I wasn't keeping up. "I tried every fucking approach. I was being sensitive with her, patient, telling her everything she wants to hear, yet she keeps rejecting me."

My mouth hung open in shock. "Vaughn."

Vaughn pointed his finger at me. "Before you say anything, I don't want another one. It has to be her."

"What the fuck are you talking about?"

He lowered his voice to whisper and barely held in his laugh. "I know it sounds like a stretch even for me, but she just won't give in so easily. However, she's one preppy, cold virgin that I would do anything to see melt in my bed."

My chest clenched, and my stomach turned in disgust. Is this how he saw her? All this time, she trusted him, and he was just trying to get in her bed? However, the feeling of relief followed. Vivi had not given up her virginity to this asshole. She had a better judge of character than me.

"You know what? Now that the frustration is out, I feel a little better." He got up and tapped my back. "Thanks."

I was mortified. Did I really choose this bastard to play Joel? This dickhead was going to play my father? Yes, Joel was reckless and an adulterer, but he never lied or cheated his way into a woman's bed. How could I have made such a mistake of casting him? What if he completely fucked up the role given to him? Did I risk too much and was now going to lose it all?

I grabbed him by his shoulder, stopping him before he walked away.

"Huh?" He turned his head, confused.

My glare bore into him. It was a silent warning that I had no intention of letting him cross that line. Vivi might not belong to me, but that didn't mean I would let anyone disrespect her. "Watch your words, Vaughn. Don't say or do something you'll regret."

He sized me up and down with a mocking smirk. "What's it to you?"

I gripped his shoulder. "If you ever mention Vivi's name in that context again, I won't hesitate to do something about it. We clear?"

He chuckled, a smirk tugging at the corners of his lips. "Relax, Tate. She's fair game."

My jaw clenched as I stepped closer. "Let's be clear," I stated, barely holding my rage back. "She's not going to be part of any games. You stay away from my main lead woman, and don't cause problems on set. Got it?"

Vaughn's smirk faltered, and I could see on his face that he deliberated pushing the topic further, but he backed out. "Just messing around, no harm meant."

I narrowed my gaze. "This is not a joke. Don't push it."

He nodded with a wary acknowledgment before leaving. I exhaled. I had little doubt Vaughn would back down easily. I would have to keep an eye on him.

* * *

"Your movie is not going to be a flop." Wade's voice resonated from the screen on my phone.

I leaned the phone on the penholder on the desk and leaned back in my chair with a sigh of despair. "I think I rushed the casting. I should have given more actors a shot to compete for it. Why did it have to be Vaughn?"

"I don't understand why you suddenly have an issue with him. I thought you could handle him?" Wade asked.

I glanced outside the window of my room. That was before I found out what an asshole he was and that he wanted to sleep with the woman I liked.

"Look, forget about that for a second." Wade snapped his fingers at the screen, trying to get my attention. "How is Flyn doing?"

I waved my hand nonchalantly at the question. "She's enjoying herself. Europe suits her."

"When Wren and I were in Europe for our honeymoon …"

"Oh god, not again. We get it. You're married. You have a wife with whom you spent a wonderful honeymoon. How long is this going to last?"

Wade closed his mouth, slightly amused, slightly irritated. "Can I finish?"

"Fine." I sigh.

"When we were in Europe, we visited Mom's house in Paris. The one she grew up in. Our late grandparents had the house kept as a homage, and it's still there. I'll send you the address. Why don't you take Flyn to see it? A little trip to Paris might cheer you up. You could use the head cooling."

"You know what?" I nodded as an idea flashed in my head. "That's not such a bad idea after all."

* * *

I glanced in the hallway. "Coast is clear," I told Flyn as we both tiptoed to the stairs. "Wait here."

I walked over to Vivi's door and knocked once. I was hoping she wasn't sleeping.

She opened her door and glanced up, confused to see me. She was wearing a pink, silk, slip dress that fell loosely over her breasts but flowed tighter over her hips and down to her ankles. Barefoot, she was even shorter and more petite than in her usual heeled stride. Her hair was pinned back with two small pins on each side of her head with a few shorter loose strands of hair at her sides. What surprised me more was her bare face. Her eyes looked wider, her lips looked softer, and she had a natural blush to her cheeks. Her hand clung to her chest, and she nervously played with the thin, golden necklace around her neck.

"Tate, what's the matter?" she whispered. "Why are you ..." Her eyes locked on mine, and the next words drifted off.

It took me a good second to remind myself why I was here. "How would you like to go to Paris?" I spoke in a hushed town.

"Now?" Her eyes widened in shock, but an excited smile spread across her face. I was distracted by it when suddenly I was nudged out of the way, and Flyn grabbed Vivi's wrist, dragging her out of the room. "Come on."

"I'm barefoot." Vivi chuckled.

"Shh." I closed the door to her room and pushed them toward the stairs. "Come on, before anyone sees us."

"I'll give you shoes in the car." Flyn giggled like a little girl, locking arms with Vivi.

"Girls, you'll get us caught." I swung the front door open, glancing back at the house to see if anyone noticed. The coast was clear. "Now go, go, go."

Once at the airport, we stepped out of the car, and I led Vivi by the hand. The airport was bathed in soft, artificial light, casting a glow over everything. The distant hum of aircraft engines and the occasional announcement over the PA system filled the air.

As we rounded a corner, the private jet came into view, illuminated by powerful floodlights. The aircraft's polished, silver body gleamed in the artificial light, its sleek lines cutting through the darkness.

Vivi gasped in amazement. "You rented a private jet on a whim?"

"Spontaneity runs in our family." I shrugged. "Snacks?"

"Champagne?" she asked curiously, looking around. The interior of the jet consisted of leather seats in deep, rich hues and a small table in the center that held fresh flowers. Next to it, there was a welcome basket.

"Aren't you underage?" I teased.

"Not in Paris." She smiled.

"My girl can enjoy herself." Flyn took the champagne bottle out of the basket, popped it, and filled a glass.

"Only one." I took the glass from Flyn and handed it to Vivi. "Promise?"

"Alright." She nodded and sat on the chair opposite of me.

Flyn sat next to me with chocolate milk in her hand.

"Chocolate milk? Seriously?" I raised a brow.

"Don't worry." She pointed at the basket. "I ordered one for you as well."

"That's the last time I give you the chance to book anything."

Flyn just shrugged and put on her seatbelt, ignoring me.

"So why the sudden need to go to Paris?" Vivi asked.

"Mom is from Paris, and Wade mentioned he and Wren went to see the house she grew up in."

"God, he doesn't miss a chance to talk about his honeymoon," Flyn muttered.

"So, I thought," I continued. "We're already here. Might as well go see it."

Vivi glanced at me. "And I'm here because I'm playing Marianne?"

Flyn chuckled. "Hon, this isn't about work. We're having fun."

"Also ..." I paused. "I wanted you to come with us."

Vivi glanced outside the window, an innocent smile on her lips. For some reason, I was getting more and more certain she didn't like Vaughn at all, and instead, she had feelings for me.

Chapter 13

Vivi

It was almost midnight, and the townhouse loomed before us as Tate, Flyn, and I stepped out of the taxi. I couldn't believe I was here, in the heart of Paris, standing in front of Marianne Blanchard's childhood home.

The townhouse was a real Parisian gem with wrought-iron balconies and fancy flower-boxed windows. Tate and Flyn had secured the keys from the housekeepers, so they took them from the little, hidden pile of decorative rocks where they were told they were going to leave them, and then we entered.

Inside the townhouse, the grand foyer had marble floors and a crystal chandelier. We turned on the electricity, and instantly there was a soft, golden light cast over the room. There were antiques everywhere and art to spare.

I glanced at Flyn. She looked all stiff like she was trying to keep it together. Tate went up to her, and I followed, feeling like a third wheel at a family reunion.

"Flyn," Tate said, all soft and comforting, putting a hand on her shoulder.

Flyn turned around, her eyes all teary. "Sorry, I know I said I'm not going to let this make me cry." She sniffled.

Tate wasn't doing better either. He didn't let a tear go, but his eyes glistened. My heart twisted as I saw their raw emotions on display.

As they pulled apart, Flyn wiped a tear away. "I miss her, Tate," she admitted.

Tate nodded, rubbing his eyes to keep himself together. "I do too, Flyn. Every day."

I edged closer, wanting to offer my support. Flyn had told me so much about her mom when we spent time at rehab together, and after playing her, I couldn't help but feel like I knew her too. She was a strong woman who raised her children right even though life had thrown so many curves at her.

Flyn turned to me, looking less choked up now. "Vivi, thanks for being here with us."

I gave a small, understanding smile and nodded. "Of course, Flyn. I'm here for both of you."

We spent the midnight hour exploring the townhouse, talking about Marianne's growing up years, and hearing stories about their mom. Every room seemed to have a piece of her character in it.

After we finally stepped outside, the air was unusually quiet.

"How about we grab something to eat?" I suggested, trying to lift the mood.

"I'm hungry, so that works. Flyn?" Tate tried his best to snap back into his chirpy mood.

Flyn stared at me for a second and then touched her stomach. "Ah, you know, I overstuffed myself with snacks on the plane. I think I'm going to head to the hotel and Facetime my friend."

My eyes widened, and I smiled at her. "Are you sure, you can just keep us company?"

Her eyes lingered on me, and I could almost swear she was teasing me. "No, no. Please enjoy Paris on your own, don't cut down on my expense."

She rushed ahead, stepped into the side of the street, and hailed a taxi. With her long legs on display, a taxi parked on the sidewalk instantly.

"Should we walk?" Tate's voice behind me sent chills down my back. I could hear my own heart drumming in my ears. Flyn had just pushed me into something that was between a nightmare and a fantasy.

* * *

Somewhere between ordering the food and the waiters getting it to our table, I had calmed down. The conversation flowed naturally, and Tate was surprisingly patient and a genuine listener. Every time I would pause, unsure if he cared what I had to say, he'd wait until I continued. For someone like me who got shunned for two years, forever saying something out of line, I was starting to warm up to him faster than I would have hoped for.

Tate was handsome, driven, charming, and everyone liked him. The more I got to know him, the more I understood why he worked well with people, but the closeness and vulnerability I was feeling around him came with the fear that this was going to crash and burn on me.

"So that's why I worry," Tate finished his sentence, taking a bite out of his roasted potatoes. "This movie is either going to be a success or a flop, but I just had to risk it. Life is too short, and if there is an opportunity in your face, the right answer always is to grab it."

It took me a second to come back to that. "Um ..." I took a sip from my water. "Why did you decide you wanted to be a producer? You could have done anything with the inheritance really."

"I had the interest long before the money came in," he answered. "Movies are worlds of their own and creating them takes a certain type of magic touch to make them great and memorable. I think I inherited my love for it from my mother. She loved to discuss movies and share her thoughts on them, whether it was good or not. I also liked how she approached critique. She said nothing is more insightful than critique. You can either take some wisdom and grow from the good parts, or learn how to be tough from the bad parts. That's why people's opinions never bothered me. But I want to prove to myself I do have what it takes to create a good movie, and I want to be satisfied with it in the end. If I like it, I believe people will like it too."

I felt a sudden chill and hugged myself, rubbing my shoulders. "Do you think Marianne learned that after her experience with the paparazzi?"

Tate took off his coat and tossed it over my shoulders. "Maybe. Probably. She didn't like talking about things in detail, rather than saying something and letting us interpret it as we'd like. Do you worry about fame and how it might influence you?"

I smiled. "Having people pry into my life? I find it awkward but not uncomfortable enough to make me stop doing it."

"Then what are you afraid of?" He seemed to be thinking of an answer himself as he asked me that.

"I fear ... being alone. No, being left alone. I also fear never getting freedom and being forever under someone's thumb. But I also fear getting that freedom and not being able to make a single choice."

"Tough situation to be in." There was a sad but understanding smile on his face. "My brother was always afraid of making a move until it was the right time while Flyn never hesitated and ended up having a lot of regrets. But both of them decided to balance things out and make a change, and they handled whatever life threw their way just fine. Trust me, you'll be okay."

"What about you?"

"Me?" A boyish grin spread across his face. "I've always felt free, and at the same time, I've been patient with making decisions. I decided to take a risk and make a movie about Joel despite most people telling me I probably shouldn't, but I also did a lot of careful thinking on how to do it."

Just looking at how confident he was, I could feel more positive about it too. "You're so optimistic about everything. I think it's one of your most awe-striking qualities," I blurted out without thinking.

Like that compliment got to him, he nervously rubbed the back of his neck and looked aside to compose himself. He turned back to me with his usual teasing smirk.

"What do you do for fun?" he asked.

Fun? I hadn't seen much fun in two years, but I figured it was too depressing to say something like that. "I read. And you?"

"So do I," he said.

"Oh really, what?"

"Gossip columns."

"What?" I burst out laughing.

"It's not my fault. My sister-in-law got me hooked on it. I read the *Manhattan Herald* gossip column once a month. She said it's a competitive spot and most of the stuff in her old column was always heavily researched since it involved powerful people. They were never scared to do some digging and plaster it in the paper for the world to see."

"Are we talking about Wren Montrose? The one who published the book about Joel?"

"She's a Blanchard now, but yes."

"I like her humor and style in the book. How is the column doing without her?"

"I think it pained Wren to confess, but she said despite the column not having her spicy humor, it's still well-researched and written."

I smiled. "I'll give it a read someday. Were you ever mentioned in it?"

He shook his head, disappointed as if that was a silly question. "I am the favorite sibling. Trust me, I get mentioned."

I leaned my elbows over the table and rested my chin over my palms, giving him a flirty look. "Then I'll definitely go and read some juicy details."

Tate locked eyes with me, and the longer I waited for him to turn his gaze away or say something, the longer the tense silence went on.

Suddenly he raised his hand and gestured to the waitress for the check.

"Let's walk to the hotel. The night is beautiful, and I'd love to hear more about you, Vivi."

Hearing my name roll off his tongue was as good as a warm breeze brushing by and caressing your face. Without showing more embarrassment, I straightened my shoulders and smiled. "Alright."

I could feel the giddiness take over as we took a walk along the River Seine. The tension and chemistry were there. Neither he nor I could deny it anymore. The glances were getting longer, the steps were getting slower, and the distance was getting smaller between us. Our hands brushed together. Every touch felt like a wave of electricity was being sent down my body. I was sensitive and on edge, yet there were no nervous jitters nor panic. I was so comfortable; everything was so easy that I just ... I took one step faster than Tate and stood in front of him.

He glanced at my smile, and then it just clicked. He leaned his frame, and our lips met. Soft, warm, and sweet. His lips traced over mine in sensual slowness while his body slowly closed the distance between us. His hand came gently over my face, brushing over my cheek. I brought my arms up to his chest, gripping his shirt's collar.

His arm wrapped around my waist, and I was pinned so close that I could feel his whole torso pressing on me. Every curve of his body, every muscle and bulge. As it sent a jolt down my body, he expertly slipped his tongue into my mouth and deepened the kiss.

I was aware of everything yet taken over by a lighthearted haze. His fingers rested on the dip of my back, his slightly overgrown beard grazing over my skin, and his taste mixed with the smell of his cologne still lingering on the collar of his shirt.

I was feeling the deep, sultry kiss tempting my body to want more. Time and logic seemed to be irrelevant. Who we were before this didn't matter. I didn't want to think, I wanted to feel, and everything Tate did felt so good. He was gentle but didn't back down. He took me a step further in the kiss. I felt my pulse quicken, my breath cut short.

Passions were building up, and soon the kiss was going to turn crimson red.

Sensing where this was going, Tate pulled back first. He brought his hand back to my face, running his thumb over my lower lip.

"You are perfect. In every way." He got distracted and pressed one more kiss before pulling away again. "Stunning." He cursed. "Shit. If I don't let you go now, someone will call the cops on us, and I don't speak French to charm my way out of it."

I buried my face into his chest laughing. "Let's go back to the hotel."

"Okay," he whispered in my ear and chuckled. "Come on." He reached for my hand, and then we walked the last few steps to the hotel.

Once we were inside, Tate and I headed straight to the receptionist. He was going to give us the two rooms Tate had booked beforehand.

"There should be more rooms booked under ..." Tate began, but at that moment, I knew exactly what I had to do.

I turned toward the receptionist and spoke in French. Tate glanced at me, confused, and I smiled. "When you are playing Marianne, a French actress, you pick up a few things."

The receptionist gave us one room key card, and I took it. "Come on."

Tate slightly reached for my hand, the look on his face quite serious. "You're certain you want to do this?"

I nodded. "I'm already having so much fun, and I don't want this night to end just yet."

He observed my eyes, and then I watched the lines on his face soften.

"Alright," he whispered and took my hand, walking us toward the elevator. The doors closed, and the bell pinged. Muffled music played in the back of the elevator.

The nervous jitters finally made their debut once we arrived at our floor. But Tate just took my hand in a strong and warm grip that sent encouragement coursing through my body. I wanted this. I wanted it to be him.

Finding the room was easy. He raised the key card, and the door unlocked. Tate pulled me along inside, and as the door closed, he kissed me.

"Tate ..." I raised my hands a bit breathlessly and wrapped them around his neck.

"No rush, baby. I will take my time with you all night." His lips ran over my face. Gentle flickers of lips over my forehead, nose, eyelids, cheeks, and then they came down to my neck.

The room was spinning, and the floor felt unsteady under my feet. I wondered if this was what being drunk felt like.

I reached for his buttons and played with them until they were all undone and I could slip the shirt off his shoulders. His biceps tightened as I ran my fingers over them then slowly dragged them to his chest. I pressed my hand over his heart, and he placed his hand over mine while he devoured me with another kiss.

It was all paced eternally slow, equally fast. The anticipation was killing me.

It was a match of give and take. The dress was slipped off my body and fell by my ankles. I was naked in front of him with no bra to shield me, but his gaze didn't cause me discomfort. His fingers played around my shoulder, and he leaned his head toward the crease of my neck. His lips ran a wet trail down to my shoulder blade. His hand gently made its way down to my breast, and he slowly brushed his thumb over my nipple. It responded to his touch and hardened while my pulse quickened. I never expected to be so excited, so impatient to feel more, to be touched like this.

He kissed me. There was an unrestrained passion in it, but everything was taken in small doses. He tasted with gusto, he enjoyed every swirl of tongue across my skin, every sigh he prompted out of me.

I was half naked, pressed on the cold wall in the hotel room, and I had barely any strength left to move farther down the hall.

"I'm so glad it's you I get to do this with," I whispered in his ear.

I felt his erection pressing on my thigh. I slid my hands down his body to his pants and reached for the button.

"Wait, wait." He grabbed my hand as if I had poured cold water over him, and he broke the kiss. "I can't let this happen."

"What?" With bruised lips and a panting breath, I was barely hanging on a thread, and now he wanted to stop? "Why?"

His eyes narrowed in a more serious look. "There's something you need to know first, and you might change your mind after hearing it."

"Can't this wait?" I could still taste him over my lips.

"No, it can't." He pressed a kiss over my forehead and then took my hand, taking me toward the bed. We sat on the edge of it, and he took my hand in his.

"You might not like what you're about to hear, but I need you to know before you make the decision to sleep with me. And if you change your mind, I will go downstairs and get that other room."

"You are confusing me."

"I slept with Coco."

My mind went blank as he said that. "What?"

He took a deep breath to gather the strength to repeat it. "Once before we came here, and I didn't know who she was, and once when we arrived at the villa. I didn't think much about it because to me it was just sex, and I think it was the same for her. I never even thought about the consequences until I realized it might hurt you."

I knew Coco liked younger men, I just never thought we'd ever have a guy in the same bracket.

"Oh my god." I ran a hand over my face. "This is bad. I can't sleep with you if you're sleeping with her."

"Vivi." He reached out to me, and I slapped his hand away, running toward the hallway for my dress.

He came after me and grabbed my elbow to pull me toward him.

"Let me go." I tried to fight him off. My vision became blurry as tears gathered in my eyes.

He took my face in his hands. His eyes glinted with regret and sorrow. "I'm not sleeping with her. It was a mistake, and I regret it now. I've only thought of you from day one. You were the one I wanted."

"Then why did you sleep with her?" I snapped.

He paused. "I don't have any excuse for what I did. I don't know what to say to make it better. I can't take it back. Trust me, I would if I could." His thumbs brushed over my cheek, and he leaned forward, resting his forehead on mine. "I'm not perfect, and I don't want to hurt people willingly. I had to tell you before we did something, but I'm really hoping this doesn't change things between us."

"It changes everything. You slept with Coco." A single tear escaped my eye, and I brought my hand up, wiping it off roughly, nudging his hand away. "Was I going to be meaningless sex too?"

"No," he snapped with a grave expression on his face. "You are not just a one-time thing. I brought you with me because I care, because you are special to me."

"How? By playing your mother? By being friends with your sister? By being young and attractive?"

"By being you!" He closed the space between us again. "You are the most beautiful woman I have ever met, and I want every part of you, but you are cold as equally as you are sweet. And you are naïve, but you're understanding because you've been through twice as many bad things as others. When you're at ease, you laugh and it's contagious, and you know just what to say to make me drop my guard around you."

The tears burned my eyes, threatening to spill, and my throat was dry as I held my words back.

"I'm sorry. I really am." He reached for my hand.

I pulled away and put my dress on. Tate's hand dropped by his torso. Silently, he moved back to the bedroom.

I reached for the door handle, but my heart didn't let me open the door. I didn't want to end things; I didn't want to let him go. A selfish need gripped my chest, and I knew it was already too late for me to back out. If not tonight, then tomorrow I would want him again. And the day after that, I would want him even more. I didn't have it in me to keep denying my feelings for him.

I walked away from the door and back into the room and saw him sitting on the edge of the bed, head hanging low. He raised his head, looking at me hopelessly.

"It was meaningless, and it's over?" My voice was already weak.

He gave me a slight nod. "I will regret it till the day I die."

I sat next to him on the bed and took one deep breath before exhaling nervously.

A bit unsure of himself, Tate reached into my lap, and this time I let him take my hand in his. His fingers were warm and gentle over mine.

"I want to stay," I said.

"I want you to stay." He held my hand but didn't make any more attempts to touch me.

We stayed like that in silence for some time, the space in the room looked brighter and wider the more the silence lingered. Eventually I rose from the bed and stood in front of him. Tate gently released my fingers, and I reached for the straps of my dress, then slid the dress down my body until it fell to my ankles.

I mounted him and wrapped my arms around his neck, my chest pressing on his. I could feel his nervous heart pounding.

"Are you sure you want this?" he whispered over my lips.

I simply nodded.

He kissed me slowly, taking my lower lip in between his. His hand glided up my inner thigh, and I opened my legs wider for him. Tate ran his two fingers over my slit.

I reached for his pants, and this time he let me unbutton them for him. He was hard for me. Desired me.

He took my hand and placed it over his bulging boxers. I could already make out the shape and size. Nervous tingles jolted at the side of my stomach.

"Are you nervous?" he whispered in between kisses.

"Excited," I answered, breathless. "But I don't want to do anything wrong."

"There's nothing you can do that won't feel good."

He gently placed his hand over mine, and he moved my hand up and down his length so I could get the feel of it and the pace he wanted me to go in.

After a few strokes, he let me take over. He began kissing my neck, but his abs tightened at my touch. He was barely holding in groans and moans, and watching him react to my touch was intoxicating.

"I want to touch every part of you," I whispered in his ear.

"Touch me however you want." He released my body and laid back on his elbows.

I tugged his boxers down until his cock was in full view. I wrapped my fingers around it, unsure how much of a grip I should have.

I glanced up at him to see him watch me with intensity and patience, giving me freedom to learn on my own.

I began moving my hand, stroking while observing him, seeing what he responded to, the pace, the grip, what he liked, what made him react.

The more I got into it, the more of his power began slipping away. His breathing quickened, and he caught my hand, making me pause.

"My turn," he whispered and then pulled me with one move under him.

I reached out and touched his face. His gaze lingered on mine, and a genuine smile curved on his lips. "Are you having fun?"

I finally could find the energy to let go of my seriousness and smile. "Yes."

He took the rest of his clothes off, taking a condom out of his pocket and placing it on.

I opened my arms and wrapped them around him as he climbed back over me. Our bodies touched, chest on chest, his hips grinding over mine. He felt warm and familiar, solid and safe. As I clung to him and buried my face into his neck, I never wanted to let go ever again.

He took his time to kiss every part of me. His tongue traced curves of me I didn't know could feel pleasure. I could see the enjoyment in his eyes, the way he wanted to touch and feel every part of me.

I closed my eyes as his lips moved lower and farther down my body until he was in between my thighs and his tongue flickered on all my sensitive parts in teasing motions.

The pleasure running through my body was exquisite.

I never thought it would be like this. I could have imagined it in a million different ways, the momentum, the person, how it would feel, but everything was better.

He slid his hands under my legs and yanked me even closer to his mouth. I was gasping for air, trying to come to terms with the ways he made me feel. And then the pleasure built up out of nowhere. I tried to ease into it, but Tate just kept me steady as he pleasured me. I couldn't outrun the feeling as it ramped over me and took hold of me. I gripped the pillow behind me and moved my hips on instinct. A trickle of sweat went down my neck.

He pulled back up, a smile curved on his face as he watched me moan my way through the orgasm.

He traced a finger down to my breast and over my nipple. "I want to make you cum over and over again. Just hearing you makes me harder."

I raked a hand through his hair with a playful smile, slightly embarrassed. "I loved every second of it. I want more of it."

He bent his head and took my breast into his mouth, sucking on it until my peeks were hard and red. "If you ask so sweetly, then you get everything you want."

He pried my legs open, and I wrapped them around him. He took his cock in his left hand and teased my slit with it.

I rose on my elbows and placed a hand on his chest, my eyes tracing every line on him.

He gently touched my wrist with his other hand. "I'll go as slow as possible." His lips came down on mine, he held my hand close to his chest, and then he pushed the first inches of his cock inside me. The feeling was uncomfortable at first, but the more he kissed me, the more I relaxed, and my body adjusted to the new feeling.

When he buried his whole length into me, he stayed there for a moment and broke the kiss to take a look at me.

His gaze was focused on every emotion on my face. The pain was minimal, and I got used to Tate throbbing inside of me, but every time he'd look at me like that, my body couldn't help but respond.

Feeling me clench around him, his lips touched my forehead and then caressed my eyes with them, the tip of my nose, then he brushed his lips over mine before placing a gentle kiss over my cheeks. "I'll make you feel so good."

He pulled out of me, leaving me unfulfilled, then eased into me again, bringing that pleasure back.

My hands went over his muscular back, all the way to his ass, and I grabbed both his cheeks as he moved inside of me. He kissed my neck, then his hands ran over my breasts, and he took one in his hand, giving it a good grope.

"Oh yes." I tossed my head back, the words slipping out of my mouth before I knew it.

His hips moved at a different angle, hitting a spot in me that made the room spin. "Yes, fuck yes." He cursed. "Don't hold your voice back from me."

He slipped a hand in between us and in between my legs, stroking me.

"Oh no, no, it's too much." I reached for his hand, but he pushed mine aside and went back to stroking me. My mind blanked out, I no longer had control over my gasps, my moans, or my movements.

I could see stars on the ceiling, my vision was getting blurry. How could it be so good?

"Hold me tighter, Tate," I whispered. "Please."

His arms wrapped around my waist in a tight grip, his movements became rougher as we rolled into the sheets. We might have been at it for hours or for minutes, but all I could feel was the pleasure and hear his moans in my ear.

His hands tangled up in my hair, every motion, every tug added to the sensation. With every thrust, he became more possessive, hungry, in need, and I couldn't get enough of everything he was doing to me.

My body reached a new level of greed too. I wanted the pleasure this man had to offer, and I wanted it to be only mine.

I was so close. "Tate ..."

"I can feel it. You are clutching onto me so tightly." His thrusts became faster, and then it shattered right through me. Long, thorough, unbelievable. Like the first satisfying burst of fireworks in the night sky, the orgasm was pleasurable, fascinating, and magical.

I pushed his wet hair out of Tate's face to see his eyes. The heavy breathing, the relaxed gaze ... he orgasmed as well. I was just too busy to notice.

"That was amazing." I chuckled, and he just smiled, settling his head between my breasts.

"I'm glad you enjoyed it as much as I did."

"I did." I caressed his hair.

"Does anything hurt?" he asked.

I shrugged. "I can't tell. You're still inside of me."

He burst into laughter, slid out of me, and lay next to me.

The awkwardness and tension was gone. It was just me and him, next to each other, relaxed and free to be ourselves.

Tate slipped a hand underneath my neck and cuddled me closer to his cooling body. "One night with me and you already have a foul mouth. I have a feeling you'd be pretty good at dirty talk."

"Mind telling me a few phrases I can use?" I rested my head on his chest. "Your favorite, perhaps."

He gave it a thought and then whispered many dirty lines I was surprised he didn't blush just saying them out loud. I had a feeling I'd need time to keep up, but the night was young, and I was a fast learner.

* * *

I woke up in Tate's arms with his phone's ringtone blasting in the hotel room. The curtains were still drawn so I couldn't make out the time.

"Tate," I whispered in his ear as he slowly woke up. I pressed a kiss on his cheek. "Your phone is drilling a hole in my head."

He chuckled and ran his fingers up and down my back. "It's going to stop soon."

The ringing stopped.

"See?" He cuddled me closer, and I lay down on his chest, trying to get some more sleep.

The ringing started again.

"Stupid time difference," he muttered and got up, reaching for his pants on the ground. He found his phone and then glanced at me with a sour look on his face. "It's Coco."

Chapter 14

Vivi

"Coco?" I raised a brow, and then it occurred to me I'd left my phone back in the villa. "Fuck, I never took my phone."

"Profanity so early in the morning?" Tate shook his head, disappointed. "You're already corrupted."

"Just answer the phone." I panicked.

He slid a finger over the screen and brought the phone up to his ear. I could hear her yelling all the way here.

"Coco, calm down, she's with me," Tate explained. "And Flyn." He was quick with that one. Coco was yelling so much, I could see the alarm on his face. "She's fine. She and Flyn are still sleeping in their rooms, we'll be back in time for shooting."

He could barely get two words in. "It was an emergency visit to Paris, so we didn't tell anyone." He paused. "Yes, she had to come with us. No, not because of me, because of Flyn. They're friends, they know each other from before." He winked at me and then grinned. "Alright, Coco. Yep, thanks for telling me. I'll go to hell. Okay, fuck you too. Yeah, see you back at the villa."

He hung up and then climbed back into bed next to me. "And she had the nerve to say you're the emotional one."

I clutched the sheets to my chest and pushed my hair back. She said that to Tate?

"What else has she said?"

His gaze told me enough.

I could feel the tension climbing back onto my shoulders again. "She talked bad about me even to you?"

He extended his hand to get me back into bed with him and then pulled me into his embrace. "Is that something she does often? Talk bad about you?"

My voice trembled as I spoke. "I wish I could say our relationship is more mother-daughter-like, but unfortunately, I can't. She is overbearing, overprotective, and exhausting. On certain days, I feel like she has it out for me rather than wanting the best for me."

"What makes you say that?"

I bit my lower lip as the bad memories flooded in. "Where do I even start? She picks at parts of me, little by little. She feeds into my insecurities; she says things that she knows will hurt me, and at times, she treats me like a prisoner rather than a daughter. I'm the constant target of her rage when things don't go according to plan, and at certain times, I think she hates me." I was finally ready to admit it to myself. "I'm just so tired of her. I am turning twenty-one soon, and the moment I do, I think our relationship will just end right there. I mean, she practically forced me to take on this role."

He listened to me carefully and brushed a short strand of hair away from my face.

"I wasn't ready for a big role," I said.

He remained calm. "Do you regret it then?"

"No, not anymore." I smiled. "Then I wouldn't have met you and be here like this."

"Good." The tense features on his face relaxed. "Because I'd be really upset if you said that you regret it."

I didn't expect Tate to be so honest, vulnerable, and sweet. "If there is one thing I regret, it's having made a wrong judgment about you."

"And what are your thoughts about me now, baby?" he teased.

I chuckled at the word *baby*. It sounded sweet.

"I'm a great lover, outstanding charmer ..." he began numbering.

"You are kind," I jumped in. "And calm and patient, which makes you incredibly more charming than charm. You understand people. And I just know that you are going to be even more incredible as a movie-maker."

I expected him to add on, smile, or laughingly accept the compliment, but he stared at me for a long time like he was trying to spot the lie. He couldn't believe what he heard. The compliment touched him more than I expected it to.

He brought his head closer and delicately brushed his lips over mine. I wrapped my arms around his torso and opened my legs, taking him closer.

Hungry passion took over, his mouth grew greedier, and we sunk deeper into the mattress.

Tate

"Why are you leaving so soon?" I watched Flyn buy a ticket for a direct flight. "You just got here."

"My agent called me with a runway offer I can't refuse, plus I think I've distracted you enough and got both of you in trouble." She glanced back at Vivi, who waited patiently while looking at the flight board.

"Just send me my things when you can and take back the rented car. All the paperwork is in the suitcase."

"So there's no way I can convince you to stay?"

She smiled. "I came here because I thought we both could use the fun and distraction, but you already have too many things to watch over. Vivi over there is glowing more than a highlight color on fashion week. I knew you were interested in her, but she surprised me. Take care of her, will you? She's already been through enough, and I really like her."

Vivi having Flyn's approval meant a lot to me. I wanted to cherish her and have her be a more important part of my life. "Of course I will. She's not a one-time thing to me."

"I know." Flyn smiled. "I can tell by the look on your face when you get serious about a girl. Not often from what I know about you, but when it's there, I can see it."

I crossed my arms. "What about you then?"

"Me?"

I leaned in. "If you think I'm obvious, you should see yourself."

"I have no idea what you're talking about."

I shook my head disappointed. "Do you think I'm blind? Carrie Campbell. Your eyes followed her around the set like a lost puppy. When you find someone attractive, you pounce, but when you like someone, you get all mushy and have this look ..."

She raised her leg and kicked my ass. "I do not."

"Ouch—yes you do!" I laughed and grabbed her in a chokehold hug. "So will you confess, or do I call her?"

"Alright, alright." She tapped my arm, surrendering. I released the hold.

"Carrie and I are friends." Flyn pushed her hair back and brushed through it with her hands. "I might have caught some feelings ..."

"Some?" I raised a brow.

"I talked to her on FaceTime yesterday and told her I was leaving. She seemed disappointed, but not in a lover-like way. I don't know if she is interested in me in that way, and I don't want to make a move unless I'm certain."

"You won't know if she's straight or not until you make a move."

"Thank you, Oprah. You focus on your girl. Are you sure Vaughn is out of the picture?"

"He was never in it." I grabbed her shoulders and pulled her in for a hug. "Have a safe flight."

"Wait!" Vivi ran toward us and gave Flyn a hug. "Text me when you land safely."

"You two are such worrywarts." She embraced her like an older sister and then released her with a pat on the back. "Go back to your villa and shoot your movie."

I wrapped my arms around Vivi's waist from behind and rested my head on her shoulder as we watched Flyn go through the security check. Flyn waved one last time before disappearing into the crowd.

"Are you going to miss her?" Vivi glanced back at me.

"Absolutely not."

A huge grin spread across her face. "You're such a bad liar."

"Come on. We got a whole airplane just to ourselves. We might as well enjoy it." I took her hand and pulled her along.

Once we were up in the air alone on our way back, Vivi sat in my lap, grinding over me while kissing me in the most sensual way a woman could kiss. Her hair brushed my cheek while her tongue traced the tips of my lips. Her small hands were resting on my chest while she impatiently grinded her hips over my lap. The dress was already up to her thighs.

I had one hand resting on her back, holding her close to me while the other one was under the dress, in between her legs, stroking and teasing her.

"You should have told me you lost your underwear in Paris," I whispered over her lips.

"I figured you wouldn't mind." She smiled cheekily.

Her laughter, the teasing note in her voice, and her blue eyes gazing at me with many things unspoken riled me up sexually more than I expected it to.

I was growing greedier for her every moment. I wanted to take it easy, slowly, have her get used to it, but she came at me with full speed.

"I underestimated you, darling. You have hot and heavy freakiness in every bone in your body." I placed a kiss on her neck. "What am I going to do with you?"

She nudged me away playfully, then carefully slipped on the ground between my legs. "Should I surprise you a bit more?"

Fucking hell. I was in heaven.

"Go ahead." I made myself more comfortable. "Surprise away."

She tugged my boxers down until my hard cock was out and in her face. I wanted to see what she was made of.

Her slim, elegant fingers wrapped around my cock, today more confidently than yesterday. She pressed the tip to her lips and then took the first half of it into her warm mouth.

"Fuck," I cursed under my breath.

As she heard me suck a breath between my teeth, she looked up at me seductively, her blue eyes under fluttering, dark eyelashes. Her movements were gentle, but she knew how to play around. She used her thumb to tease my tip before taking all of me back into her mouth and pulling back up with a grin on her face.

My chest tightened, and I gripped the leather seat while she kept taking it in her mouth. I thought she'd be shy and coy, but she wanted to please, had an eagerness, and she was ready to explore. I tangled my fingers in her hair and nudged the back of her head toward the base of my cock. She took the encouragement and picked up the pace and how deep she took me.

She had me moaning and groaning, moving my hips, thrusting into her hand and mouth, and urging her to go faster. I could feel my orgasm building.

"Yes, baby, yes, keep going. I'm about to come," I managed to blurt before she focused her mouth just to suck on my sensitive tip, twirling her tongue around it. It was enough to violently shove me over the edge, and in a matter of seconds, I held her head over my lap, burying my cock deep inside her throat.

As I came into her mouth, I released the grip on her head and opened my eyes. Her eyes glistened with choked-up tears, but the look she carried on her was one of a sultry woman who had just achieved her goal.

"I'd love to see you swallow my cum." I caressed her cheek.

Without a second thought, I watched her swallow and then wipe the sides of her mouth. In a teasing manner, she stuck her tongue out at me to show me and then climbed back into my lap.

I was too stunned for a good second. My emotions were a wreck, going back at forth between wanting to protect her and hold her to having her orgasm under me.

"Was that good?" Her innocent gaze was back. "I knew what I was doing in theory, but it's my first time."

I closed my eyes, taking a deep breath to calm down my quickened pulse and beating heart. This woman was going to be the end of me.

"I'd put a ring on your finger for that blowjob alone." I winked at her, and she hit my shoulder, amused by the thought, then she settled back into my arms.

I held her close, wondering about that myself. Why did the thought of putting a ring on her finger sound more satisfying than any other thing recently?

"Am I part of the mile-high club now?" she teasingly asked me.

I smiled. "Not yet, but we can fix that. You just have to straddle me."

She mounted me and grinded over my cock, getting me hard again. She took my cock in her hand and slid it back at forth. She was wet for me.

I grabbed her waist and wrapped one arm around it while I used the other one to guide her where to place my cock.

Her eyes were on mine, warm and friendly, so damned attractive in the way they looked direct and deep into mine.

She took me inside of her, nice and slow, and common sense rolled out the window.

I touched my lips lightly to hers, and she responded with a kiss, warm and aroused. The taste of it, the sharp demand of it, pushed my sanity away.

I arched my hips, and it only took one moan to have me driving deeper. Her fingers tangled in my hair, and she opened her mouth to me.

She moved over me with a tremble and then began rocking over me. I had to tear away my mouth from hers and press it to her throat to keep myself from rushing both of us. The natural scent of her skin mixed with the spring fragrance shampoo from the hotel was like a shocking snap to my system. It tormented me and got my pulse racing.

Moment by moment, her body loosened, and every gentle thrust she took as she rode me was building up in her.

There was excitement in her eyes as she was not able to catch her breath and control her voice. At this point, even the pilot would have heard her.

My mouth came greedily back on hers, and she returned the kiss, running her hands over my shoulders, down my chest, her fingers gliding over the muscles on my stomach.

I took pleasure in watching her enjoy herself. The slow, tortuous movement was detaching me from reality.

I picked up the pace and thrusted until I was deep inside of her with every plunge. I skimmed my fingers down to her breast. Her lashes fluttered, and she looked at me in anticipation.

I slipped my hand inside her dress and skimmed my thumb over her nipple.

"Oh god." Her breath caught, and her eyes closed shut.

Her moans became short whimpers as I pulled her dress farther down, and then her breast spilled free. I lowered my head, devouring it in my mouth. She began moving restlessly, sinking her fingers to the base of my head to ease the feeling.

It made me want to tease her more. I held her tightly pressed to me with my hand on her waist and then began moving more roughly. She tried to break free, but I held her there, trapped with no choice but to endure the sensations.

I released my mouth off her breast and looked up at the desperate look on her face. She was close, and I could also feel her clenching down on me, begging for an orgasm.

A few last thrusts, her body convulsed, and a wave of pleasure took over her. She shuddered in response and collapsed on my chest. Her muscles went lax for a moment, and she took one breath before a muffled scream left her lips.

"The orgasm won't stop," she pleaded over my lips.

Her pleasure pained look made my blood boil in my head, heart, and cock. I had no plans on letting it end here.

I moved again, and this time I pressed her close to me, arms trapped. She writhed and cried out until she shattered again in another orgasm.

My breath hitched as I quickened the tempo, hard and fast, before slipping out of her and under her, and then I came. My body spun out of control, and I felt my cock twitch and throb as it spilled down on the ground.

Neither of us said anything but let go of control and laid in each other's arms for a while.

Chapter 15

Vivi

Half of the crew was already in action when we arrived. They were setting up for the next scenes while Vaughn and Elena were practicing their lines. Tate gave my hand a last squeeze before running off to find the director and see where they were. Off the hook for today, I headed upstairs for a good bath while trying to contain my giddy mood.

As soon as I walked into my room, I saw Coco sitting on the bed, arms and legs crossed. She got up and walked over with a glare on her face. I instantly knew she would not be lenient.

"Wait, I can ..."

She didn't let me get the rest of the sentence in. Raising her hand, she slapped my face so hard it echoed in the room. I could feel the heat rising to my cheek, and soon the pain followed. My eyes filled with tears.

"You don't shit where you eat!" she yelled. "I have told you that a million times, and it's the last time I'll have you embarrass me like this!"

The hate in her eyes was evident. A cruel and cold stare that I knew had nothing to do with worry out of love and everything to do with pride and ego. Like needles prickling my skin, her words always found a way to hurt me.

"How dare you leave the shooting site and not even tell me?!" She was looking for an excuse.

I couldn't say anything. The words were stuck halfway in my throat barely, holding back the sob.

"Oh, I see, you don't want to talk." She folded her arms under her chest. "You're fucking the producer now, so you're a big shot?"

And then I could see it. The jealousy on her face. She hated me because she thought I stole something, someone that was her right. I was a prude in her vision, a girl who had no power over a man unless she told me what to do and how to do it. If it involved someone she thought might profit her like Vaughn, I was encouraged to do it, but if it meant getting close to her interest, then I was going to be shamed for it.

I knew there was nothing I could do. Like every other aspect of my life, there was no way I could fight her.

"I can see it on your face." She grabbed my chin forcefully. "You fucked him, didn't you?"

"It was a one-time thing!" I blurted out, tears pouring out of my eyes. "I just wanted to have fun. Didn't you tell me to loosen up?"

How could I say anything else when she was ready to take away everything? She had more than enough power to do so.

"Then swear on it!" she ordered. "Swear that you'll stay away from him. I don't want you fucking up your appearance in this movie."

The very thought of it was like a burning pain. My throat clenched, not wanting to let the words out.

"Well." She released my chin, waiting for me to back down as I always did.

Knowing she could rip my heart out, use my real feelings against me, and destroy me, I cowered and lowered my head. "I'll stay away from him. I'll make an excuse."

Only a few more months, and I'll be twenty-one, I told myself. A few more months and she would have no more financial power over me. I would be free to properly be with Tate. I just had to hide it for a while and keep him at bay.

"Good." Coco knew I would wield under pressure.

She pushed her hair back and walked over to the door. "I'm going out with some of the crew and extras who aren't needed on set for drinks."

"You want me to come?"

She smirked. "Oh no, you had enough fun. You'll stay here as a punishment for running off to Paris."

I wasn't sure what she meant by that, and then I saw her slam the door shut.

I rushed over, trying to get it to open, but then I heard the lock click. "No, Coco! You can't do this to me! Not here!"

"I can do whatever I want. That will teach you a lesson about doing things without my permission."

I heard her walk away as her heels clicked on the wooden floor. "Coco! Please! I'm sorry."

Isolation was the one thing she loved punishing me with. Her rules were simple: You listen to her, you get freedom; you don't, and you can be locked up for days.

I threw myself back on the bed, tears streaming down my face. My pillow soaked up my tears. I couldn't see Tate anymore. If I did, god only knows what Coco might do.

Chapter 16

Tate

It was impossible to forget about her for a single second. I could still taste her sweetness on my tongue, feel her gentle caress over my skin, hear her moans in my ear. I was drowned in the constant replay of bodies intertwined and how she looked when she'd orgasm. I couldn't focus as the thought of pleasure had a stronger pull on me than ever before.

It wasn't about going after the feeling with anyone. It was experiencing it with her, not sure I would ever get enough of kissing her.

I tried my best to get the scene down by 8 p.m. It was already dark, and the stars had come out. Director Giles was in need of a drink and got the rest of the crew together. He turned to me.

"Let's go grab some drinks. I heard most of the cast and crew already went out."

"Um ..." Did that mean the villa was empty?

"Everyone from the cast?" I asked strategically.

Giles absentmindedly thought about it. "I assume everyone except Vivi. I think she never left her room."

She was probably resting from the night before as she did have a lot of adventures to recover from. A smile curved on my face. If we were going to be alone in the villa with no one around, the choice of having her wherever I wanted was thrilling. I began wondering if she was thinking about me in the way I was thinking about her all morning. I wanted to hear her voice, hear her say how much she couldn't get me off her mind.

"Are you coming?" Giles asked.

"I might join you later. I have some things to finish in the office ..."

"Oh, come on. We worked all day; we need a break."

"Tate's not coming?" One of the crew members sighed, disappointed. "You're the life of the party, come on. The first round of drinks is on me."

"No, I can't." I raised my hand, but Josie walked over, overhearing the conversation.

"Come on, Tate, what's the hold-up? Not handling alcohol like you used to?"

I waved them off. "Go and enjoy, have fun. I might stop by later."

"Suit yourself." Giles sighed.

"You're not fun." Josie pouted.

I waited for Giles and the rest to get out of the villa, and then I rushed upstairs to Vivi's room. I was ready to knock on the door when I heard smothered cries.

I leaned my head toward the door to make sure I heard right. She was crying. My body broke into a cold sweat.

I grabbed the handle, trying to get in, but the door was locked.

"Vivi, it's me. Open up." I banged on the door.

The crying stopped, and then I heard her footsteps as she approached the door from the other side. "I can't."

"I need to look at you. I can hear you crying. Open the door."

"No, I can't," she cried. "Coco locked me in here. I don't have another key."

She did what? The anger took over my body faster than I could control it. "Okay baby, hold on. I will run downstairs."

"Don't leave," she cried out. "Tate, please."

"I'm just going downstairs to grab the spare keys from the office. I'll be gone just for a minute."

I rushed downstairs, running toward the office. I pushed papers away and tossed them aside, trying to find the keys under the piles of documents. Eventually, I spotted them, grabbed them, and then ran back to her room.

As I unlocked it, the door swung open and Vivi came out, tossing herself in my arms.

I pressed her closer to me, wrapping my arms around her and holding her tight. "Shh, it's alright." I kissed the top of her head.

Her body was trembling in my arms as she sobbed. She looked weaker like this, more fragile. It was as if after the ice melted, all there was left was this feather-light girl who barely held onto me.

"It's okay." I rubbed her back, repeating the words to her. I noticed she was wearing the same dress as this morning.

"How long have you been in there?" I asked, fearing the answer. "Have you been locked up all day today?"

Her shoulders relaxed, and her sobbing slowed down. I felt her loosen her grip on me, and she pulled away to look at my face. Her eyes were wet and swollen, and her face was stained with tears. Her gaze slowly began changing in front of me.

From someone who was desperate to have me here, to a grief-stricken resolution on her face, and then her cold demeanor was back. Her eyes became a void of emotions.

Changing the topic, she nudged me off and took a step away from me. "Thank you for getting me out of there."

"Were you in there all day?" This time my anger slipped out. Was she locked in her room as punishment for spending time with me? Was she treated this way because of me?

I could see the hesitation to answer in her eyes before she decided she was going to run away. She rushed toward the stairs. "I need some air."

"Where are you going?" I stammered.

"Don't follow me."

The words pierced me. The confusion that had been building inside me now churned into a storm of emotions.

"What did I miss? You were clinging to me a second ago?"

She turned to face me, gripping the stair rail. Her eyes were filled with tears again. "What happened yesterday was a one-time thing, okay? It can't happen again."

Like hell it was. "A one-time thing?" I managed to utter. "Come back here and explain to me what's going on."

She rushed downstairs.

Oh no, she was not leaving after dropping this on me. I ran down the stairs after her. She leaped through the hall and went straight through the French doors toward the pool. I managed to catch up just before she passed the pool. I grabbed her wrist to stop her from taking another step and pulled her back toward me, wrapping both arms around her.

She tried to wriggle herself out. "Let me go." Tears streamed down her cheeks now, and she trembled. "I don't want to continue seeing you."

"You're a great actress, but a terrible liar."

She began panicking, her eyes looking around to see if anyone was watching us.

"It's only me." I held her back to my chest and whispered in her ear, "It's just you and me, as always."

"We can't be together," she finally snapped.

I released her and turned her toward me. "Is it me? Is it fear of intimacy or getting close to someone?"

Vivi shook her head in denial, looking down. "No, it's not that. It's ..." She hesitated, finally meeting my gaze with an intense vulnerability.

And just like that, I knew what the problem was. She was not the type to burst into anger but one to cave under it.

"It's because of Coco." I ran my hand over my face. "I should have known. What is wrong with her? You're not a child."

"Don't you think I know that? But my life is different. You don't understand how my relationship with her works."

"Coco should mind her own business."

"She owns me until I'm twenty-one!" She took a shaky breath, her tears unabated. "She controls me. She always has. I can't go against her wishes."

"So, you'll just do whatever she wants, even if it means sacrificing me."

Vivi's shoulders slumped, and she took a step back, creating distance between us. "You don't understand. I wish you did, but you don't."

My frustration was growing. "You are just going to give up?"

"Yes." She turned her head away.

"If you're going to turn me away, then at least look at me when you say it."

Her body was trembling as she tried her best not to cry. She couldn't look me in the eyes.

I reached out for her and took her trembling fingers in mine. "For me, it cannot be a one-time thing. I can't let go of you. Especially when I know you don't mean any of the words you say."

She closed her eyes briefly as if gathering her strength. When she opened them, she had her old, cold look on her face. "I don't feel the same way. What do I know? I'm just a naïve girl who was a virgin until last night and I ..."

I closed the distance between us and kissed her. She turned her head aside, and I brushed my lips over the soft skin below her ear.

"I hate you. I hate you," she repeated.

"There is not one cruel bone in your body that would make me believe that."

She shuddered with a sob and turned her head, finding my mouth with hers. I stroked her hair, her cheeks, as my lips softly lingered on hers.

"I'd never hurt you," I whispered over her lips.

"Coco, she—she's controlling in ways that you can't even imagine."

"Just for one moment, don't think about her."

Her gaze lowered to my lips, and her hands finally reached out to my face. "I wanted to touch you like this all day. I desperately thought about it."

That was good enough for me. Desperate, I closed a hand over her breast and let the hunger take over the kiss. Her taste pumped through me like good alcohol. I wanted this to be slow and sweet, but she began moving restlessly in my arms, tugging and pulling on my clothes, trying to get me out of them. I couldn't think, I couldn't breathe. It was all taste and sound.

Her dress came down on the ground while she struggled with my belt.

"I need you know," I demanded.

"Take them off." She released her grip on me.

I battled my way out of my pants, and as I tried to kick them off, I staggered backward. In an instant, I lost my footing and fell into the cold pool.

"Tate!" I heard Vivi's laughter drowned by the sound of the water in my ears. I broke through the surface, wiping the water off my face.

"Shit, that's cold."

"Are you alright?" She had broken into a smile.

"Why are you laughing?" I splashed water at her, hoping to make her laugh more. "Help me."

She reached out her hand, her laughter echoing in my ears. When she touched my fingers, I pulled her in with me.

Water splashed everywhere, and she broke out of the surface, laughing. "Traitor."

I clamped my mouth onto hers. She wrapped her arms and legs around me and accepted it. Her restraints were gone. I carried her to the stairs of the pool and rose out of it, laying her down on the cold tiles.

She ran a hand thought my wet hair with a pleading look on her face.

I lowered my head and took her breast in my mouth, sucking on her nipple. It perked in my mouth as I swirled my tongue around it. She was damp, yet hot and thrilling. I squeezed her breast again, desperate and needy to be inside of her.

My right hand slid back down over her hip, down to her inner thigh. I traced it up, slowly, until our eyes locked. She jerked against my hand as I eased a finger into her. She was already ready for me.

I stroked her with my thumb and placed a kiss in between her breasts. She whimpered and moaned, the most beautiful sound I'd ever heard.

I felt her thighs clenching rhythmically for something not yet within her grasp. Like lightning that struck within me, I had to have her in the same moment.

I slipped my cock into her and watched her cry out in shock, in delight. She dug her fingers into my shoulders, and her eyelids closed halfway. Her eyes, a dark blue tonight, never left mine. She was seeing only me, she wanted only me.

I burrowed against her and took her mouth in mine. I brought her arms over her head and intertwined my fingers with hers. My breath was coming fast, and my blood was pumping hot. I was greedy for her, more than I had been for any other woman. I wanted more from her. All of her.

Her rosy damp skin, small curves and breasts, and how sweet she sounded moaning in my ear. I could feel her tremble under me, gasping for air and losing control over her senses.

She was beautiful, breathtaking. Even when she was vulnerable. Even when she was being ice cold. Even when she was sweet. I loved every part of her, every response.

I was falling for this woman, and there was no wall in the world I couldn't tear down for her.

I drove inside of her, faster and stronger, until she quivered beneath me. I could hear my name, but I was lost in thought and feeling. Maybe it was her eyes that drew me in or because her laughter was infectious. Maybe it was the way I found myself wanting to be the one to brush the hair from her face or hold her when the world seemed to weigh down on her. Maybe the feelings grew the more her smile had a way of brightening up my day and being around her made this whole thing feel so easy. In her company, everything else seemed less important and more important at the same time.

I couldn't stop, not yet. Not until I was completely consumed by her.

She pleaded with my name on her lips while I thrusted into her. It was long, relentless, harder. Then her back arched as the second orgasm overtook her.

I released her arms as I pulled out of her, spilling everything over her glistening belly, then collapsed breathlessly over her. She brushed my wet hair back as I laid with my head in between her breasts.

In the back of my head, I knew I should get up from the cold floor and get us dressed before we got caught, but I couldn't let her go. I wanted us to just lay together as much as we wanted, with no one to break this moment.

"Tate." Her soft voice lingered in the air.

I gathered the last strength I had in me and rose to meet her eyes. All my defenses were gone. I was willing to gamble everything to have her, with no anchors in the shape of wrong decisions and regrets making things impossible for us.

"We should get up." She smiled with ease.

I let her slip away, and I watched her get dressed. She brought a towel over and kneeled next to me, playfully drying my hair with it.

My muscles were loose, my brain foggy. I found myself staring at her, wanting her by my side, mornings, afternoons, and evenings. I wanted all her days, both good and bad.

"Why are you looking at me like that?" she asked as she folded the towel.

"Just because." I managed a smile.

She helped me up, and we get dressed and sat down on one of the chairs by the pool. As she lay in between my legs with her head resting on my chest, I felt a comfortable flicker of home. I leaned back and closed my eyes. She wrapped my arms around her waist and covered my hands with hers with a good squeeze.

The night seemed so calm. The air was silky cool against my skin. "You're a sin," I murmured. "A beautiful one."

That made her laugh as intended. "And you're a flirt."

My arms strapped tight around her. My stomach flipped with a nerve-wracking feeling that this was one of those fleeting moment that passed ever so quickly, one remembered on lonely nights. I couldn't shake off the fear of this being the last time I could hold her like this.

"What are you thinking about?" Vivi asked after the long silence.

"Nothing." I kissed the top of her head. "And you?"

"I was thinking that this is a night I will remember even on the worst days to come." Vivi turned toward me with a smile that was almost bittersweet. "Thank you for being everything I could hope for."

I touched the tip of her nose, the nervous feeling twisting deep in my gut. "Now, why does that sound ominous?"

As I said that, I heard heels clicking over the cobblestone path.

Chapter 17

Vivi

Coco walked in on me and Tate together, and the moment I saw her calm expression, shivers ran down my spine. She was too quiet for someone who forbade me to see Tate only a few hours ago.

"Guess Prince Charming unlocked you, and you willingly walked over everything you promised me." She reached the pool and crossed her arms.

Tate and I awkwardly got up from the chair.

"Coco," Tate spoke. "I think you need to take a step back here. Vivi's not a child and—"

"You stay out of this," she snapped at him. "This is a family problem, and outsiders have no say in it."

"Don't talk to him that way." The loud voice left my throat without thinking, but I couldn't stand to hear her talk to him that way.

She grabbed my wrist and yanked me along with her. "We will talk in private."

"Let me go." I tried to yank my hand out, but it was useless.

"Let her go!" Tate yelled after her.

Coco sent him a glare. "You come closer, and she is the one who'll get the bitter end of things."

That stopped Tate right in his tracks.

"Vivi." He turned toward me, waiting for any instruction if he should interfere.

"It's fine, I'll talk to her." I gave him an encouraging smile and walked with Coco inside the villa.

Her grip on me didn't loosen until we reached my room. She pushed me inside aggressively.

"You're going to lock me up again?" I yelled at her.

She scoffed. "Oh, you learned to bark, how cute. Now shut up and listen."

"No, I'm done listening to you," I yelled. "You keep acting this way and think I'm going to put up with it forever. Well, I've had enough. I've given you so many chances, and you keep crossing all my boundaries. I'm done taking your shit." I pointed a finger at her. "I will never understand how someone can be so cruel and indifferent toward a person. Have I not done everything I could for you? Was I not good enough of a daughter, always doing your bidding and everything you've ever asked me to do? I've always found a way to try to understand you and your ways, but lately, all I feel is that you are this cruel person who never cares about me or my feelings. You keep pushing and pushing until I break, and even then, you keep at it until I fall off the edge and lose myself."

She crossed her arms, completely unphased. "Done now?"

"No, I'm not even close." Tears gathered at the corners of my eyes. "I'm human, and I make mistakes, yet you never let me forget them, and you even punish me for them. You've forced me to become someone I hate, and I can't sleep or eat because I am constantly reminded of all the things I'm bad at. I can't live like that anymore, and I don't care if you think it's unfair, but I'm not letting you manipulate me into it again."

"Is this his doing? One day with him and you're acting like this? Like a useless brat who hates someone who knows what's good for her," Coco said.

"Stop it!" I yelled. "Stop trying to turn the situation in your favor as you usually do. I'm not your puppet. I'm not something on a string you can control however you feel. I'm done. I don't want to hear it."

"Look at you, look at what he has done to you!" She clapped her hands. "He ruined you."

"He didn't do anything but show me care and love, unlike you, who's never known more than to hurt and to insult."

Her bitter laugh resonated throughout the room. I watched her in complete shock and disbelief.

"Stupid and naïve little Vivi." She kept laughing. "Love? Are you talking about that sleazy idiot who sticks his cock into every girl he can? Love? Please."

"Tate is not like that," I jumped to his defense. "I know that you slept together and that after he broke things off with you, he rushed into things with me, but I'm partly to blame here as well as I initiated it."

"He doesn't love you, he only wanted to fuck you, darling. Wake up to reality."

"If this is about jealousy, then ..."

I knew it had been a mistake to say it the moment the word was out of my mouth. Her glare became intense and fear-evoking as she took one step toward me. "Jealousy? You are so far away from my level to even say such a ridiculous thing. The only thing you're worth is a cheap tabloid picture of your adventures in that pool slapped with your name on the cover to sell some gossip."

My breath got stuck in my airway. "Excuse me?"

"I saw you and Tate in the pool a while ago," she said. "How funny it is to think you got upset when we even suggested you're a slut but you're fucking like that in the open."

I barely pieced the words together. "What do you mean you saw us?"

"Not just saw you, I have proof." She took out her phone from her back pocket. "I have all your dirty actions on camera, and I will sell everything to the highest bidder since you don't want to play nice anymore and do what I tell you. If you wanted me to be the bad guy, then you should have just said it from the start, sweetheart."

"How can you be so cruel?"

"It's just business at the end of the day."

"Tate will never let you do this."

"Hah." She laughed out. "You have to be fucking kidding me! Your sweetheart, the man you think loves you and will play your hero is nothing more than a porn star."

"What? It's ludicrous to even …"

"I mean, you have to be pretty fucking stupid to believe anything that comes out of his mouth. He works with actors; you think he can't tell a lie when he needs to? Men will say anything if it gives them a chance to fuck you, and you fell for the oldest trick in the book. You don't even have to ask him, do a little dive on google, and his low-budget, pathetic, indie porn movies will eventually pop up. That is how much your hero cares for you. That look on your face is pathetic, but even you know that I would never claim something so boldly without having the proof to back it up."

Tears were already falling down my cheeks, and I got stuck in a sob. "He would have told me."

"You are naïve. And going against me while listening to that bastard is the stupidest thing you've ever done. You will regret everything soon, however. Making me your enemy will not go unpunished. While everyone is already used to watching Tate Blanchard fuck on camera, 'Virginal Vivi,' the prudish Astor heiress will be a sensation. It will be the most searched title, and as always, all your pathetic little fame and success will be because of me."

So, when he told me about past mistakes alongside sleeping with Coco, about things he couldn't change, he was talking about this? And not once did he think to tell me.

Did he purposefully hide the truth from me? Was Coco right? Did he only tell me things that were convenient for him? Even when he saw how much I valued his honesty, he looked straight into my eyes and made the decision to omit the truth and lie to me.

I silently fell to my knees. The betrayal followed by the pain of humiliation and crushed pride in front of a woman who hated me and wanted to take everything away.

Coco wasn't going to stop there. If she had a video of me, I didn't doubt that she would use it. The thirst for revenge and need to control me was more important than her ruining my life.

If I wasn't with her at the top, then I had to be discarded to the bottom. I was just a money bag to her, the stories she sold me were cruel lies too. She never cared either. That was also manipulation on her part. And now I was going to suffer in front of the whole world again, my most vulnerable self out in the open for people to see.

"God, you're pathetic." Coco turned on her heels, leaving me a mess on the floor. She walked to the door, leaning over the door handle. "Don't worry. I will give a piece of my mind to your boyfriend too. I just can't wait for the press to get a hold of the story as I tell them all about the man who is just like his late father. A troublemaker, scoundrel, and an adulterer. The one who ruined 'my little girl' and made a pure girl into a loose woman over the span of a few months. I could write a book and sell a sob story about a mother who didn't manage to protect her child from a man like him."

The words "her little girl" were the last straw. A pierced cry left my chest, and I turned toward her with all my rage thrown out. "I am not your little girl. And you are certainly not my mother. You have never, ever been my mother, nor will you ever be."

I rose to my feet, my vision blurry and my legs wobbly. "If she hadn't died when I was a baby, I never would have gone through this, and you would never have the chance to treat me and hurt me the way you did."

Coco had no emotional response on her face. The person in front of me was a stranger.

When dad brought her home for the first time, I thought she was so beautiful. I looked up to her, wanting to be like her when I grew up.

She had spent most her time in the house, avoiding me the first few years, until I had made it my mission to get her to love me. I thought she didn't feel accepted enough. I wanted to make her feel like we were family.

So, I followed her lead. I told Dad I loved leaning on her. I trusted her advice, I stayed out of her way. The more Coco fit into the household, the more left out I felt. The more control she gained, the more I lost it.

But that didn't matter because Dad was happy, and I was happy for him.

Then in the moment he was gone, any shred of Coco's kindness was gone. I tried and tried to survive on the little crumbs of affection she fed me, believing that she was still family and I couldn't lose her as well. But tonight, I could no longer go on.

"How can you live with yourself?"

"Did you think I was going to cry?" She headed out the door. "Too bad your real mother is dead then."

The door slammed shut behind her. I stood there trembling while grief poured over my body. I had tried my best to believe Coco was a second chance at a mother in my life, but it was all a lie too. I had deluded myself into thinking she could ever care about me even if I accepted her.

While I played along, didn't dad ever doubt what kind of person he was marrying and entrusting his daughter with?

I walked over to the door and gripped the handle. I was pathetic, crying over something crying wasn't going to fix. Coco was going to get what she wanted whether I despaired over it or not. But air and comfort were hard to reach. I invincibly moved my body and opened the door.

No matter how humiliated and betrayed I felt by Tate, I had to see him, I had to talk to him. I couldn't handle this on my own. I dragged my heels down the hall to his room when I heard Coco's voice again. Only I couldn't believe what I heard this time.

Chapter 18

Tate

Coco entered my room looking as smug as ever. My glare locked on her as she took a few steps closer to me.

"She has you wrapped around her little finger, and you let her." Coco crossed her arms. A smirk curved along her face. "You are just as easy to fool as the rest of them."

I placed my hands in my pockets and sighed. Unbelievable. I was a fool to believe anything she'd told me before.

"Listen, Coco, I'm doing this out of respect for Vivi. If you don't pack your bags and leave the set this instance, I'm no longer going to play nice. You do not need to be here, and while so far, I've allowed you to stay, for god knows what reason, I think it's time you go."

Her smile was gone. She didn't appreciate my condescending tone or the glare.

"I think not," she snapped back. "I'm here for Vivi's sake, remember?"

"After what I just saw, the fuck you are. I have no intention of letting you near her if I can help it." I reached for my pocket, taking my phone out. "In fact, I think I'll make a few calls now to deal with you."

"You do that, and I will scream." She smiled wickedly. "I will spin the narrative on you before you can even spell harassment. You already took advantage of poor Vivi. You corrupted a sweet, innocent girl trying to make it in the industry, and you with your newly found money exploited your job as a producer."

"You fucking ..."

"Bitch?" She nodded. "I'll take it as a compliment. After all, there is nothing I wouldn't do for my daughter."

"How can you say that when Vivi is willingly with me and will continue to be with me? You are underestimating the public's judgment of common sense, and they will see right through your bullshit."

She scoffed. "You and I both know if Vivi was normal, she would, but she is not stable; she has mental health problems. I, as her mother, accompany her everywhere because of it. I want to protect her until she is better, but you took advantage of her vulnerability and naivety."

"Stop saying that nonsense, even as a joke."

"Oh, it's finally getting through to you!? I can ruin you faster than you can even imagine, baby. You are, after all, a man."

"I've heard enough. Get the fuck out."

She didn't even flinch. Almost as if she was provoking me to grab her and drag her out so she could make a scene. She was insane, deluded that she could get away with everything.

"Get out," I said through gritted teeth.

She took a step closer to me. "You are hilarious." She laughed in my face. "Do you think I'll get scared and run? I don't see you as anything. To me you are just a pathetic man who was once a porn star and now is desperately trying to be something he is not. It's not you who wrote the script, it's not you who shoots it. The actors, the staff, everything is done on their backs. You didn't do anything. You just tossed your money at them. That's all you're good for. Daddy's money."

For a second, it stung. All my hard work, the vision, pulling everything together and trying to pave the way for everyone to make this movie was tossed out the window in a second. Yes, I invested money in this, and others used their talent to make it come true, but it was my vision. I consulted, studied, helped, and did tons of research to make everything go smoothly. Not that this woman could appreciate it or understand it. It was funny how all my life I had to work hard for things and scrape for things to make them work and nothing was enough without money, but now that I had them, money overshadowed everything.

Daddy's money? I was grateful for it, and I made damn sure I spent it, but it wasn't as harsh of an insult when all my life I wanted to have someone's back to lean on.

"Say whatever you want, but unlike you, Joel knew what it was like to be a parent who can take care of his children."

She laughed again and shook her head. "What are you talking about? Then again, of course you'd be blind to it, as you are just like him. Joel Blackwood was nothing but a womanizer. You are exactly like him. You fucked whatever was available here; as long as it kept your dick wet, it didn't matter if it was me or innocent Vivi. You can put as many pink filters on the script as you want to make Joel seem redeemable in the movie, but he was just another man whore, and that's what you are too."

I clenched my fist and withdrew a breath. "Whatever you are trying to provoke me to do, it's not going to work."

"I think it's working. You seem a little tense. But that was never my intention, baby." She closed the distance between us and leaned over my chest. "I wanted to give you a little idea of what happens if you cross me and don't stay away from Vivi."

I leaned over her. "Not going to happen."

"I'm pregnant."

The words echoed in the room, and my stomach clenched in panic. I'm sure I heard wrong. Why would I care if she was pregnant?

"My period was late, so I checked." Her eyes narrowed, implying something I didn't want to believe. There was no way I got her pregnant.

"The baby is yours. I only fucked you while I was here, unlike you, who twiddled around."

"I was careful, there is no way ..." I panicked. I was sure I was careful every time, but the last time my head was a mess, I didn't even think to check the condom.

"It's yours," she repeated as if to rub it in. It was all a joke to her.

"If you're lying about something like this," I warned her.

"Even I wouldn't lie about something like that."

"No, no." I grabbed her shoulders. "There's no way you are pregnant."

"I can prove it." She smiled.

I felt the strength and conviction leaving my body. This wasn't happening. I tried to wrap my head around it, but denial took over. I gripped her shoulders. "You can't be a mother. I see the way you treat Vivi, you are ..."

"Congratulations. You are going to be a dad." She grabbed my neck and pressed her lips on mine. I blacked out for a second in shock.

No! Not a fat chance. As I pushed her away, I heard a sob. My head snapped toward the door to see Vivi covering her mouth, her eyes wide open and teary.

"She's pregnant and it's yours?" The look in Vivi's eyes was one of betrayal.

I stumbled over my words. "I haven't ... it's not ..."

"Yes, I'm pregnant." Coco suddenly wrapped her arms around my waist and leaned her head on my chest. "Are you going to congratulate us?"

Vivi let her arms drop by her sides. She was speechless. Heartbroken. Rage and sadness flashed through her eyes. She didn't even spare me another glance. She turned around and left.

"Vivi!" I yelled after her.

"Get out of my way," I heard her yell at someone in the hall.

I pushed Coco off me and went after Vivi, but she grabbed my elbow, using all her strength to stop me.

"Before you go after her, I think you need to meet someone special I invited just for you."

I glared at her. Was she serious? I had no plans of meeting with anyone until this whole chaos was fixed and I talked to Vivi.

Then the door opened farther and I saw a man standing there. The resemblance was there. Tall, dark hair and tanned skin. Nathan Valletta, my exiled half-brother was standing there looking smug and pleased with himself.

Coco finally released my elbow. "We have a proposition for you."

"We?" I turned to her. The moment I saw her looking at him, I knew immediately. They were in on something together, and it wasn't going to be good.

Chapter 19

Tate

Nathan Valletta. He was my half-brother as much as Ethan was. He was also one to grow up without Joel as a father figure, like me and my siblings, only he was equally included in the Blackwood family even while Joel was alive. Joel gave him money and a vote in the company, and he went so far as to publicly accept him knowing his own reputation was already damaged as it was having so many marriages and divorces. Unlike Flyn, Wade, and I who only learned of Joel after his death, Nathan had time to meet him, bond with him, and be part of the family.

He had everything I had wanted.

Yet in the few years he had with Joel, Nathan had managed to make Ethan his sworn enemy and spend a fortune of Joel's money on cars, boats, mansions, gambling, drugs, failed investments, and strip clubs. He tried to vote out Ethan from the company he helped build, and then he used Ethan's wife's brother to ruin her company at the time for his personal gain.

Reaching out to him did nothing but provoke him. He wasn't interested in making peace with Ethan nor bonding with any of us. Flyn, Wade, and I were enemies to him as we already diluted the inheritance he wanted to get his hands on.

Money and power were his drive and motivation, and without need for any of us, Wade, Flyn, and I had decided to side with Ethan and shun Nathan.

I hadn't heard from him until we got here, and rumors were flying around about him and his wife Valesca, Vivi's cousin, possibly separating. I didn't want to know or care, so what was possibly the reason he was standing here with Coco Astor?

I was a pawn. This was a game. The more I thought about it, the more it made sense. They wanted to use me for something, and they'd cornered me.

"So, I assume this is not going to go well for me?" I placed my hands in my pockets. Fucking pricks.

"No, it's not." Nathan glanced at Coco and then back at me. "I heard about the happy news. Congratulations on the baby."

I scoffed. "Are you kidding me? The way I see it, it has got to be yours."

"Of course not. He is married." Coco made an innocent face, acting in front of me to prove her point. "Us, on the other hand, we had some fun times together."

I shook my head. "No one will buy that crap."

She walked over to Nathan. "Nathan and I practically never met. No one has seen us together either. But some of the filming crew already know that me and you were fucking in the guest house, Tate. I made sure they knew."

I tried to remain calm. "What is it with you two and your perverted schemes?" I turned my gaze to Nathan. "Didn't you pull the same crap once before?"

Nathan's smug smile was replaced with a glare. "Only this time, I'll make sure it's successful." He grabbed Coco's neck from behind and pulled her in front of him. Nathan whispered in her ear, "Be a good girl and tell him what we want from him."

She glanced back at him, turned on by it.

I scoffed at them. "Speed it up, will you?"

Instead, Coco turned around, kissing Nathan. If I was not as pissed off, I would have rolled my eyes at this.

"Anyway," Coco turned toward, me wiping the corners of her lips, "I will pull Vivi from this movie, and it will be easy to do so as she hates you now. Then I will tell the press I am pregnant with your child. And then to make sure you understand your position, I will leak your sex tape."

"My sex tape? I lived as a porn star for quite some time. You do realize how ridiculous this sounds to me. Post whatever you want. I don't care."

"I forgot to mention Vivi is on it too. You two really know how to enjoy a pool."

She recorded Vivi and me by the pool? That's what she meant by sex tape?

My chest clenched at the thought of Vivi getting hurt more than she already was. Would she really do that to her? "Why would a mother do that to her own child?"

Vivi rolled her eyes. "Oh, enough with that already." She pushed her hair back, irritated. "God, both you and her really know how to make a person sick with a word. She's my daughter in name only, but I am the closest thing she has to a mother, so if I say there's no bad publicity, then that is what she'll learn from me. You need to get your nose out of other people's business."

My head felt heavy with the new information. I didn't expect to feel the anger take over when Coco bluntly said she was never Vivi's mother in any way. As the words spilled from her lips, I felt a cold rage creeping up within me.

Coco was staring at me with nothing short of entitlement and indifference. Did she look at Vivi like this all this time? When Vivi told me how she had been treated, I couldn't imagine a mother doing that to her child.

But then I remembered Slade and how in the worst moments in our lives, he was never there. He dipped out, and then every time he came back into our lives, he claimed he loved us as a father.

I knew well enough there were parents who didn't love their children. It made me feel sick to imagine how Coco must have treated Vivi. Like an inconvenience or a tool to be used. She never once felt guilty. I didn't even know how she justified it to herself.

Vivi being betrayed by Coco like this probably broke her heart in two. Not to mention I was part of that betrayal now as well.

My fists still clenched as I took a step closer to Coco. The eerie calmness in my anger made her take a step back. I had to get this over with and find her.

I loomed over her, my voice remained steady, and my gaze didn't waver. "What do you want?"

Coco shifted uncomfortably, and her indifference wavered, replaced by a hint of anxiety.

"We want what's rightfully ours. You are going to get Ethan's lawyers to back away and give Nathan his rightful inheritance from Joel's estate. Also twenty percent of the film's takings, plus shares in Blacksite."

"Those are mine anyways." Nathan pushed Coco out of the way. "If I don't get my birthright the easy way, then I will get it the hard way. That's what you get for siding with Ethan."

"We sided with Ethan 'cause you are a prick who would have discarded us as soon as you got what you wanted."

"Doesn't matter now, does it?" He pushed me back. "You know what?" He pointed his finger at me. "I knew you'd be the weakest link. You'd crack easy under pressure, and when given no way out, you'll be smart enough to know what's good for you. Give me what I want, and you and your girlfriend can have your happily ever after as soon as she turns twenty-one."

So that's why they did this. Coco would eventually lose control of Vivi when she turned twenty-one, and all the money and everything her father owned would go back to her and

Coco would be left with crumbs. She needed income, and she decided to generate it in the worst possible way.

She used Vivi to get to me and then got pregnant. Whether the baby was mine or Nathan's, I still had no way out of this without hurting Vivi. Everything had worked out for her even more perfectly now that I was in love with Vivi. Coco had killed two birds with one stone—she'd found a way to get rich as well as destroy her stepdaughter.

"You have twenty-four hours to decide, Tate," Nathan warned me. "It's either I get a happy ending, or no one gets theirs."

Chapter 20

Vivi

I was having another panic attack. I couldn't breathe or see anything in front of me. I almost tripped coming down the stairs but fell into someone's arms. The scent of "Sauvage" cologne seemed familiar.

"Woah, are you okay?" Vaughn gripped his hands on my shoulder as I raised my head to look at him. "Why are you crying?"

"I don't want to talk. Please." I tried fighting him to release me. "Let me go."

"I can't just leave a crying girl alone." He took my hand and pulled me along into the kitchen.

I was too overwhelmed to argue. I just wanted to forget what I saw. I never knew it could hurt so much to see two people kissing, but having been my stepmother and the man

I loved in each other's arms was more than I could handle. I wanted to scream in rage.

"Do you want to talk about it?" Vaughn took out two mugs and then took out whiskey.

I rubbed my eyes and face, drying it from the tears.

"Here." Vaughn passed me one mug filled with whiskey. "You look like you need it."

I grabbed the mug from him and chugged the liquid down. It was bitter and hot, and it burned my throat. I placed the mug down, coughing. "One more."

"It's not a shot, take it easy." He took the mug from me and then went to refill it.

I didn't care if the whiskey killed me right then and there because I was already dying on the inside.

"Don't go chugging this one now too," Vaughn warned as he handed me the refilled mug.

I took it, glaring at him. "I'm done listening to others."

I brought the mug up in a cheers motion and then downed the rest.

Vaughn watched me drink it, and surprisingly, he stood there with me in silence.

Bitterness rose to my throat, threatening to choke me. My body felt cold, my muscles stiff, and I could feel a chill creeping down my back. I wanted to drown in numbness and let myself sink into it instead of feeling this way.

Confusion, fear, pain. It kept stabbing at my heart, and I couldn't run away from it. I couldn't rationalize it. It hurt too much.

I placed the mug on the counter behind me and closed my eyes. It had been some time now, and I didn't hear Tate nor Coco come down the stairs.

Were they celebrating? Why wouldn't he come after me?

My heart was pounding. How could I think this way when he got Coco pregnant?

My head started spinning, and I leaned backward to stay firm on my feet.

"I thought it took time to feel the effects of alcohol." I was getting dizzier by the second. "Vaughn, are you sure this was alcohol? I don't feel good." I pressed a hand on my forehead to fight the nausea and sleepiness that took over. My limbs were beginning to go numb.

Vaughn approached me and slipped a hand around my waist, pinning me to his body. I lifted my hands to push him off, but I felt my energy slipping away.

"It's not the alcohol," he whispered in my ear. "But don't worry. I will make you feel better instead."

I felt a sudden chill of fear run down my back before I completely lost consciousness.

Tate

I sunk into a sitting position on the bed, resting my elbows over my knees while my head dropped down. I could feel the blood rushing in. I was in trouble. There were more things at stake here than just me. I had to think of my family as well as Vivi. I didn't want to let anyone down.

I couldn't just discard the fact that Coco was pregnant. A large portion of me knew the baby was probably Nathan's and she was using it to get to me, but I would have to take a DNA test to be sure. It was already bad enough to think that woman wanted another attempt at being a mother when the first attempt as Vivi's mother had horribly failed.

Thinking of Vivi made it only more painful. There was also the video Coco had of me and Vivi being intimate. I couldn't let that video go public. It would destroy Vivi. I had to protect her somehow, but Ethan, Wade, and Flyn would take the hit if I just agreed to Nathan and Coco's requests.

Self-pity was not going to help. I had to find Vivi first and talk to her, clear up any misunderstandings, and see if there was a way to make it work with her despite everything. Particularly after what she witnessed, I doubted she wanted to have anything to do with me again.

I knocked on the door to her room, but there was no answer. I opened the door, but the room was empty. I began searching for her in the other rooms, but she didn't seem to be anywhere. Did she leave the villa?

I took my phone out and tried calling her, but nothing went through. Her phone was off.

How was I supposed to find her? There was a nagging fear that ate away at me. What if Coco said something more to her? What if Nathan got to her too?

That thought left a pit of despair in my stomach. My desperation was growing. The thought that she might have left with Nathan and Coco gnawed at me, but imagining something bad could have happened felt like I was losing the most precious thing in my life.

Frantic, I called the last dialed number in my phone.

"Aren't you too busy to be making late-night calls to your sister?" Flyn was chirpy as always. "You should be spending time with Vivi and making her come ..."

"Flyn, be serious for a second!" I snapped and then sunk down on the couch in the living room. "I'm in trouble."

Flyn remained calm. "What happened?"

"I can't find Vivi. Something happened. Coco, she ... she thinks she's pregnant."

"What?" Flyn yelled. "Oh my god. That must have shocked Vivi."

"Coco also claims it's mine."

I could hear her gasp. "No way! You're careful, you always are."

"I know, but ever since I came here, I've been so stressed with filming and Vaughn ... I didn't check any of the condoms."

Flyn paused before clearing her throat and asking the next question. "And Vivi, how is she handling that information?"

I paused, and Flyn cursed.

I closed my eyes. "I know it's bad. It's really bad. But it gets worse." I told her everything that happened tonight and how Nathan was involved in this as well.

Flyn brimmed with anger. "Listen to me. We cannot let them blackmail us like this. I'll call Wade and Ethan. We will work something out."

"I know, but I need to find Vivi first. I need to talk to her."

"Beg for forgiveness too."

"I think it's a little too late for that."

Flyn yelled into the phone, "You find her and talk to her!"

I clenched the phone in my hand. "I can't reach her phone, and I can't find her anywhere. If you can just come up with some solution that I can't think of right now ..."

"Fine." She calmed down. "I will try calling her. Maybe her phone is not off and she just blocked your number. Give me a second."

After she hung up, every passing moment felt like an eternity in hell. Finally, Flyn called me back after a few minutes.

"Well?" I clenched the phone in my hand.

"There's a problem." Flyn's voice carried a worried note. "I couldn't reach Vivi, so I called Carrie. Luckily Carrie saw her. She said she came back into the villa because she had too much to drink and left the team dinner. Before entering the villa, she saw Vaughn carrying Vivi princess-style into the guest house. Tate ..." She paused. "You don't think Vivi is riled up that much that she'd go and sleep with Vaughn, do you?"

"She wouldn't do that even if she was angry at me. Thanks for this, Flyn. I owe you big time."

"Go find her; we will deal with everything later, together."

I hung up, rushing down the stairs. Something felt wrong, I could feel it in my gut. Vaughn carrying her just didn't make any sense to me. I had to find her.

Chapter 21

Vivi

I awoke in the dimly lit guest house, my head spinning and my thoughts scattered. I jolted up into a sitting position. I was in my underwear in the middle of the bed in the guest house by the pool. Confusion clouded my senses, and I wrapped my hands around myself.

Why was I naked? How did I get here?

I tried to recall how I ended up in the guest house. I remembered taking another sip from the alcohol and the way it bitterly tasted and torched my throat, and then there was the hazy memory of Vaughn's face right before I blacked out.

I suddenly got shivers down my spine. The one glass couldn't possibly have made me this dizzy. Panic and anxiety surged through me as I clutched the edge of the bed. My heart raced, and I forced myself to sit up, scanning the unfamiliar room for any signs of danger. My inner alarm was going off. I had to run. I rose from the bed, only to stumble back as my head pounded with an ugly headache and my legs still felt numb. The realization that I might be in serious trouble tightened its grip on my racing mind, making everything worse.

"You're awake." Vaughn suddenly walked from behind the bed and showed up bare-chested in front of me, finishing a glass of whiskey and placing it down before approaching me.

I moved back on instinct. "Why are you naked? Did something happen?" Tears gathered in my eyes. "Did you do something to me while I was unconscious? Where are all my clothes?"

He shook his head. "Sleeping with someone unconscious doesn't turn me on." He extended his hand, reaching me. I moved out of his grip, but he grabbed my wrist and pulled me closer. "I was waiting for you to wake up so we can have fun."

"I need to go." I tried to get out of his grip.

"Don't run away, beautiful, I'll make you feel good."

"I don't want this. Give me my clothes back." I tugged my wrist back, but his grip was strong. He just wouldn't budge.

Vaughn wrapped his other hand around my waist. "When I saw you crying, I knew it had something to do with Tate. After yesterday's trip in Paris, you fucked him, didn't you? But he doesn't deserve you."

My eyes filled with tears.

"Shh." Vaughn embraced me and placed his knee between my legs, nudging me to fall on the bed, and he climbed over me. I felt his wet lips on my neck. "I will make you forget about him."

I pushed his chest with the little strength I had. "I don't want this. Get off me!"

"You'll start enjoying it soon enough."

"Get off me!" I screamed.

"Stop fretting so much." He suddenly grabbed my face. "Just be pretty and do what I tell you to do."

I was in real danger. I had to scream. Before I knew it, I was screaming his name. "Tate!"

Vaughn covered my mouth. "He is probably fucking your mom at this moment. Everyone knew from the start they were sleeping together. When I saw you getting closer these last few days, I had a feeling you'd give into him too." He sighed. "Doesn't matter that he ruined you. I still want you." He tried kissing me.

I turned my head away. "No."

He kissed my neck again. "I want you so much. I've never craved a woman this bad. Just give in."

My body responded with disgust. "Let me go!" I screamed again.

The door of the room was kicked open, and then Tate fell in.

"You are bothering us. Get out." Vaughn smirked at him.

Tate's rage seemed to lock on the target. He immediately jumped forward and tackled Vaughn off me and to the ground.

Chapter 22

Tate

I thought I heard her scream. The door of the guest house being locked was odd enough. I kicked my way in, but once I got inside, saw Vivi in tears and half naked, I blanked out. Next thing I knew I was pummeling Vaughn on the ground. "I'm going to fucking kill you."

Vaughn's face twisted into a malicious smirk, his eyes glinting with a sadistic pleasure as if he had expected this confrontation. Blood dripped down his nose.

"She wanted it." He laughed.

Vaughn's laugh was a taunt, and it was enough to trigger my rage. Without another word, I swung my fist at him again, aiming for his face. The punch connected, landing squarely on his jaw. I felt the sharp jolt of pain as my knuckles collided with his skin, but it was nothing compared to the fury I felt.

Vaughn fought back. He pushed me off and stood up. He wiped the blood from his split lip and retaliated with a wild swing of his own. The punch grazed my cheek, stinging as it made contact.

I had no control over myself anymore. With a burst of adrenaline, I lunged forward, tackling Vaughn to the ground. We rolled on the floor, grappling and landing punches. It was chaos, an uncontrolled frenzy of fists and fury. I could taste the metallic tang of blood in my mouth, but I couldn't relent.

Finally, Vaughn seemed to realize the gravity of the situation. He kicked me in the stomach and then slid away, getting up on his feet and running away.

"Let him leave." Vivi rose in a sitting position, barely any strength left in her to walk. Her eyes pleaded with me to end the violence. She was safe, and that's what mattered most.

But I couldn't let Vaughn go. I ran after him, managed to reach him at the poolside, and grabbed him by his shirt. I pulled him back and then punched him one more time.

Vaughn took an ill-timed step back, stumbling on the pool's edge. He teetered for a split second, his arms flailing for balance, and then he tumbled backward, plunging into the pool with a splash.

I waited for him to burst out of the water, but he wasn't coming out.

"Tate, he's drowning!" Vivi yelled as she stumbled out of the guest house barefoot.

I should let him drown for all I cared. Instead, I jumped into the pool. My clothes clung to my body as I swam toward

Vaughn. The water was surprisingly cold, and the adrenaline pumping through my veins drove me onward. I grabbed Vaughn by the shoulder and hauled him to the surface.

I managed to get him out of the pool. Vaughn lay there unconscious, bruised, and battered. With a racing heart, I knelt beside him and checked for a pulse. There was none.

"Did he die?" Vivi fell on her knees beside me.

"He is not dead yet. Can you go inside to call for an ambulance?"

She nodded through sobs and wobbly stood on her feet.

I tilted Vaughn's head back gently to clear his airway and leaned down to listen for any breath. There was none. I only took this life saving course in case I needed to help Flyn when she was still mixed up with drugs; I never thought I was going to use it to save this useless piece of garbage.

I pressed my lips to his and exhaled two quick breaths, watching his chest rise slightly with each attempt.

Vaughn remained unresponsive. I started chest compressions and pressed down with all the force I could muster. One, two, three ...

After a series of chest compressions and breaths, Vaughn finally sputtered and coughed, water spilling from his mouth. The relief that surged through me was overpowering. He was alive.

The color gradually returned to Vaughn's face. Exhaustion took over me, and I collapsed into a sitting position next to him. Four minutes later, an ambulance arrived.

The EMT attacked me with questions in French that I couldn't keep up with. I struggled to answer, but Vivi came out of the villa with a shirt on and Carrie by her side. Carrie approached the paramedics and took over, trying to explain the situation.

I heard one of them telling her to call the police, and then they took Vaughn on a stretcher. Carrie went with them, and Vivi and I were alone again. The silence between us was deafening.

I rose to my feet and looked at Vivi pleadingly. "Vivi, I ..."

Her tiny hand was raised, and then it came straight down to my face in a strong slap.

"No! You don't get to say anything." Tears leaked through her lashes as she wrapped her arms tight around her body.

"I know I have no excuse for my past job, and this pregnancy—"

"Enough!" she roared, and I could see the anger in her eyes. "You and your lies, I've had enough of them. I don't care about who you've slept with in the past, but you took me to bed knowing that you might have gotten Coco pregnant."

Nausea and panic rushed through me. "I didn't know. I was careful. I—"

"You were inside me!" Her rage sliced through anything I wanted to say. She raised her hand and slapped me across the cheek again. I neither defended myself nor evaded the blow. I couldn't. I deserved it.

"Do you know how that makes me feel?" she snapped viciously.

Nothing would have prepared me for how she looked at me. Hate, disgust, resentment.

"I don't even know if the baby is mine." I tried to reach out to her, but she jerked away.

"You can't know, and until you can, don't even dare to touch me."

"I'm sorry, I'm really sorry."

"No! You don't get to be sorry."

I knew that. I fucking knew there was nothing I could say or do to change her mind.

"I'm trying to come to terms with this situation myself. It's not even Coco who is making the shots. Nathan is. They are blackmailing me."

Her brows narrowed in confusion, and she took a step back. "What? Nathan?"

"My half-brother."

Her eyes widened in surprise. "The man I crossed paths with before in the hall, was that him?"

"Yes."

She was silent for a moment before she raised her hands, pushing her hair back, and then she let her hands rest on her neck. When she looked up at me, she had a resolved look on her face. "This was a whole fucking plan, wasn't it? That's why she insisted on coming here. That's why she pressured me for this role. She needed to get to you somehow, and now she even offers me as collateral to get you to do her bidding."

I clenched my hands into fists at the urge to touch her. I couldn't. "I said I won't let her hurt you, but she managed to get the better of both of us. I broke my promise to you. But not this time. I will fix this, I promise."

"No, no." Vivi shot a cold glare at me. "You had your chance. This time, I will deal with her."

"I mean, it's not just her anymore. Nathan and Coco, both of them are blackmailing me with the video of us in the pool. They are threatening to release it if I and the rest don't give shares of the company and twenty percent of our inheritance to them. I am going to be fine, but I can't let them do it to you."

"Coco is going to regret everything. I'll make sure of it." Her voice trembled, but her eyes burned with an unwavering resolve. "I'll deal with her this time and bring an end to this."

"What about us?"

She remained silent, swallowing the heavy lump in her throat. She pointed at the cut under my eyebrow that had been throbbing in pain for some time now. "First, let's take care of that."

Chapter 23

Tate

I was leaning on the kitchen counter while Vivi sat on a tall bar chair and balanced herself as she tried to sterilize the wound under my eyebrow.

I watched her study my cut, observing it as she disinfected it. She had a stone cold look on her face.

"When I first told you about Coco, I did it because I thought it was the right thing to do. When I kept quiet about my past in the porn industry, it was because I rationalized it to myself that if I told you later on, when you cared for me, you'd be more accepting of it. It was self-serving, but I wanted you too much to be fair. I'm sorry for that."

"Stay still." She gripped my neck, pulling me closer. Her face stayed unsmiling. She didn't want to hear me out.

My fingers trailed the cold counter as I tried my best not to reach out to touch her.

"Nothing I can say can fix this, I'm aware of that. You trusted me, and I fucked this up."

She slapped a band-aid on my wound and then began shoving things back in the emergency kit box. She avoided looking at me directly. "There is nothing you can do if she's pregnant. Nothing you can do if it's yours. And there's nothing you say that will erase the hurt you caused me."

Her voice quivered, so she bit down on her lower lip to steady it. She drew a long breath. "And I'm aware this it's not entirely your fault."

"Oh, it is."

"Are you not angry my stepmother is blackmailing you and your entire family? I'm the one who brought her to you. Without me, Coco never would have had the chance to do this."

"None of this is on you." Bitterness clogged my throat. "I'd rather you hate me than blame yourself for it."

"I hate Coco. Right now, more than ever. I hate her for everything she has ever done to me, but I hate her for giving me a reason to hate you too."

"You should."

"But I can't."

I watched her as she struggled to keep her emotions in check. She gripped her chest and drew another breath. "Why should I be cheated out of my chance for happiness? Why should I let her steal another thing from me?"

"I don't understand." I didn't think I had any energy left in me to be shocked.

"I want revenge, and the best revenge against Coco would be to be so happy and live such a fulfilling life that her presence would be just a vague memory."

She slid off the bar chair and walked away. I was stunned, struggling to absorb the shock, but I got myself together and stormed after her, catching her in the living room. She stood there, her hands slightly trembling.

I was one step behind her, watching her back, and I was too afraid to reach out to her again, but her words meant something, didn't they?

"Can you repeat what you said again?" I asked.

"I thought I was pretty clear." She said louder. "Why do I have to be alone? Why would I need to suffer for your poor judge of character and for falling for the tricks of that woman?" she snapped at me. "Do you understand? I want to be happy away from her."

"But I don't deserve you."

"Huh?" She vibrated with fury. "Are you going to do the honorable thing now? Are you going to join that woman and give her what she wants? Because if you want to walk toward her or take the easy path, just leave, then I can hate you. Trust me, I have it in me to learn to hate you if I have to. Do you want to walk away?"

My voice barely had strength left. "No."

"Then it's settled." She pressed her hands on her hips and took one breath of relief. "I'll get my revenge with you by my side."

My knees gave out, and I lost my balance. Vivi reached forward, holding me steady. "Are you alright?"

"I was not ready to hear you say that."

"Yes well, me neither. But I'm stubborn and persistent, and I want to be happy."

My throat felt rusty, but I managed to come up with a few words. "Does this mean I can touch you now?"

"Aren't you touching me already?"

My eyes stayed on hers. I couldn't believe she'd be willing to let this go. Was I lucky? Did I earn the right to be happy too?

She touched my cheek with her hand and nodded as if she could read my mind. My arms wrapped around her, gently at first, then tightened, tightened until I buried my face into her neck. Emotions overwhelmed me as they got a firm grip on my heart. I drew in her scent, calming my rapid heart down.

"I'm happy with you," she said as she held the back of my neck. "No matter how crazy it is, I'm happy, and I don't want to let this happiness go."

"I'll do anything to let you keep it." I pressed my lips on her skin. "I swear to you."

"Vaughn," she said heavily.

"I'll fire him and slap a lawsuit in your name," I immediately said.

"What about the movie? We need to resume filming as soon as we get back to New York. What are we going to do?"

"I will deal with him. He will never come close to you again. I'll make sure of it."

"And the crew? They will ask what happened."

"It's none of their business if you don't want to tell anyone what happened."

"I don't care if the rest know. In fact, it's better if they do. I want the world to know what kind of a person he is."

"Vaughn is gone. I'd rather not have someone like that play my father, and I don't want him ever going near you again."

"You promise?"

I closed my eyes, still gripping onto her tightly. "Yes. I'll protect you and keep you happy forever, I promise."

"It would be a better promise if you kissed me to seal it."

I brought my head up and crushed my lips over hers in a searing, greedy kiss. Even as the moan strangled my throat, I kissed her and held her with all my might. I didn't want her changing her mind.

She turned her head away, reaching for air. I pressed my lips to her cheek.

"I'm not going anywhere, Tate. I've already made up my mind."

I brought my lips back on hers, gentler this time. She responded as willingly as the very first time and let me kiss her until we were both too wrapped up with one another to think about tonight's problems.

* * *

Carrie had pulled through for me and Vivi the next day. The villa was in an uproar with everything that happened. When I had talked to Giles and Josie about wrapping up the remaining scenes in the villa without Vaughn and moving the shooting back to New York, they were hesitant at first. Carrie, however, supported me and Vivi and even said she wouldn't work with someone like Vaughn. To our surprise, Elena had supported the decision, referred to Vaughn as a creep who needed to get fired, and even agreed to reshoot scenes with a new actor if it came down to it.

After that, the whole cast was on board, and we moved on to shooting the last few scenes without Vaughn.

I was worried about Vivi, especially after the events of yesterday, but she was the most relaxed I had ever seen her. She even spoke to most of the crew without reservation for the first time. The moment she decided to just cut off Coco, a huge weight seemed to lift off her shoulders.

Vivi said she had a plan, but she had yet to tell me what it was. Instead, she asked me to focus on the movie and leave the rest to her. I suppressed the urge to push her for information and decided to trust her on it.

I watched her from the side, slightly worried, slightly at ease.

"She'll be fine. It's the first time she took the initiative to talk to everyone on her own." Carrie approached me and handed me a cup of coffee.

She glanced at Vivi. "Little by little, she'll get more independent and trust herself more to act on her own without Coco's influence."

I took the coffee and raised a brow. "You seem to know a lot more about her overnight."

"Sorry, I pushed Flyn to tell me." She turned to me. "Vivi was attacked by Vaughn, and Coco was nowhere to be heard from or found yesterday. I knew something was off immediately. I called Flyn, and she told me some things."

"I never thanked you. If it wasn't for you, I wouldn't have found Vivi in time."

"For once, my bad alcohol tolerance paid off." She smiled. "I had such a headache, I don't think I would have answered the phone if it was anyone else except Flyn."

"Lucky." I glanced at her and couldn't help but tease her. "You and Flyn seem to have gotten pretty close in such a short time."

Carrie suddenly looked taken aback and embarrassed. "I mean, yeah. She's cool. And nice."

"Nice?" I raised a brow. "Are we talking about the same Flyn here?"

"Yes." She laughed. "She's been nothing but sweet and kind to me. She even told me if I ever need a good time in New York, she knows all the good spots."

"Well, I wouldn't put that past her. She certainly knows New York like the back of her hand, and she always has free passes to any show. Even before we were known to the public. Model perks."

Carried nodded. "She is really gorgeous. So weird she's single. She is single, right?"

It was so subtle and innocently asked that to the untrained eye, it would have seemed like such a normal question. I knew there was potential for something more between them. Flyn was worried if she was straight, but I just had that feeling. Carrie was always lowkey and private about her life and showed no interest in dating, but when she met Flyn, she showed interest to her more than anyone else on set. There was something there more than friendship, and I was willing to bet on it. Plus, messing with my siblings and their love lives was a hobby of mine.

"Flyn is single." I brought the cup to my lips. "No boyfriend. Or girlfriend." I took a sip from the coffee and glanced at her.

Carrie couldn't suppress the happy smile upon hearing the news.

"You know what? To thank you for everything, I'm thinking of throwing you a party when we get back to New York. Flyn will be there too. How does that sound?"

Carrie wasn't a party person. In fact, she was known to never attend red carpet parties or anything that wasn't needed. If she said yes, then that meant ...

"I would love that."

A smirk curved on my face. "Perfect."

Exactly as I thought.

Suddenly Vivi rushed over, excited clutching the phone in her hand. "I'm ready to tell you the plan now."

Chapter 24

Tate

The moment the shooting came to an end, we threw a party to thank everyone for their hard work. Josie had handled the details like catering and went as far as to call a DJ. The party was thrown by the pool, under the open sky, the bar was refilled with drinks, and lights were put up. She had taken the idea and worked miracles with it.

The cast members were lounging on the plush, cushioned couches, clinking glasses filled with champagne. The air was filled with music, laughter, and the sounds of the Mediterranean waves hitting the shore under the villa.

Vivi and I clinked glasses, and then I walked over to the DJ booth, asking him to lower the music for a moment. It was as if nothing had happened to upset the peace. I raised the glass, getting everyone's attention.

"First, before I make my speech, let me just say that if making movies were as easy as celebrating on the French Riviera, I'd be out of a job. But luckily, we've got this incredible crew who turned hard work into an absolute blast."

Everyone laughed and cheered.

"Now, I'd like to thank the phenomenal crew and the actors. You've put up with more drama behind the scenes than any of our characters, and for that, we salute you."

Josie broke into laughter the most and then raised her glass to me and Vivi. "While this is far from over and we are continuing our shooting back in New York, I'd like to celebrate these few successful weeks we have spent here and to thank you all for your support."

As everyone cheered, slowly the applause died down and everyone turned toward one person. Vaughn had appeared, and he seemed to be confused about the party. His face was bruised and swollen from yesterday's fight, and unlike his usual behavior, he approached me like a dog with its tail between his legs.

"I came to apologize." Vaughn approached me and turned to face everyone. "I know I caused a lot of trouble for everyone. I don't know what you heard, but ..."

Everyone was on edge. Carrie walked over to Vivi and placed a hand around her protectively. "There is one person who you owe a big apology to."

"You're right." He attempted walking over to her, and I extended my hand, blocking him from making a single step forward.

"You can do the apology from here."

"I'm really sorry for what happened." Vaughn touched his chest as if this pained him. "It's a sickness. I have a sex addiction, and this time, it came out full swing. I had no idea what I was doing and that it was nonconsensual. I swear."

Sex addiction, my ass. "There, you apologized. Now get out of here. You are fired."

"What?" He turned to me. "Come on, Tate. I will get into therapy; I will take pills. Why waste money on reshooting scenes and hiring a new actor? The public already knows it's going to be me."

"Did you not hear me? You are fired. Pack your things and leave. Also buy your own plane ticket back. I'm not paying for you."

He grabbed my elbow and leaned forward. "What do you need me to do? Beg?"

I knew he was already on thin ice and his agency was going to drop him if he got in trouble one more time.

"Get on your knees and beg then."

Vaughn was taken aback. His grip on me tightened, and then I saw him grit his teeth as he got down on his knees.

Everyone was still and quiet. Vaughn waited for approval. He had to seize every opportunity or his career was over. He was going to keep quiet and beg if that's what it took to save his career. But that was his problem.

I leaned over him and gripped his hand, removing it from my arm. "Not even if you bark will it change my mind."

Vaughn picked himself up from the ground and then stormed out of the villa. I gave the security I hired a look, and they made sure to follow him out.

Vivi walked over to me and wrapped her arm around mine. "It's time."

I glanced at the entrance to see Coco and Nathan coming from the same road Vaughn had just left.

"Alright everyone, let's continue the party." I gave the DJ his cue, and he turned up the music again.

We both approached Nathan and Coco. I took Vivi's hand and observed Coco's reaction. Her eyes remained on Vivi, who was glancing down at the ground submissively.

"Let's talk in private." I glanced at Nathan.

"Do you have the shares ready?" he asked.

"I have everything ready," I answered through gritted teeth.

"Good." Pleased to hear that, Nathan took a step back and pointed toward the villa. A smug smile curved across his face.

Vivi and I led them inside where the music was muffled and it was easier to talk. Coco observed Vivi like a hawk while Nathan took a leisured seat on the couch and slid a finger into his collar, loosening his tie. "Let's see the papers then."

Coco sat right next to him and crossed her legs, tapping her finger on her knee. "Before that, I saw no announcement that Vivi is taken off the movie."

She wanted to get a reaction out of Vivi, get her to look up. "I want her fired."

I crossed my arms. "That is not going to happen."

She straightened her back, shooting a glare at me. "That wasn't part of the deal."

"If they give us the shares and the money, what does it matter what she does?" Nathan tapped her thigh.

"No," Coco was persistent. "I want her off the movie." She glanced back at Vivi and smirked. "She needs to pay for disobeying me." She finally turned to Vivi. "Don't you have something to say? I'm surprised you forgave Tate after everything, but then again, you were always docile and a little slow."

Vivi raised her head, tears streaming down her face. "Why are you like this? What did I ever do to you to have you treat me like this? How do you think I felt with all the emotional and physical abuse I endured all these years? It was one thing when Dad was alive, but it only got worse after he died. If you had shown even a little amount of care and love, I never would have spiraled."

"Are you blaming me for your mental problems?" Coco scoffed. "How convenient for you. If you want someone to blame, blame your father. He saw everything yet had nothing to say about it. If I was that bad, do you think your own father would have allowed it?"

Vivi wiped her tears, but more poured out. "How can you say that? Dad's only fault was believing only the good in people, and I tried to honor his memory thinking you could be a decent human being. But I was wrong. You never changed. It only got worse. Don't you have any sympathy for anyone?"

"I have sympathy. For you." She grinned. "I warned you to stay away from Tate, but you didn't listen. If you hadn't disobeyed me, you never would have gotten hurt in the first place."

I rushed over to Vivi as she began wobbling on her feet. She clutched my hand to remain standing.

"However," Coco leaned forward, "if you beg me, then I won't throw you out of the house before your birthday." She crossed her legs with a smirk on her face. "Or you'll go from an heiress to a homeless woman, if I decide so."

"Are you really going to blackmail us like this?" Vivi asked, her voice trembling.

"I'd even sleep better," Coco answered.

The room got quiet. I released Vivi, and she tossed her head back up, getting the hair off her face, and she wiped her tears with a calm expression.

I watched Coco's face twist with confusion.

"God, those tears looked real." I clapped my hands and turned to Vivi.

She sniffled and dry patted her face. "Thanks."

"You faked those tears?" Coco was so blatantly shocked, she rose from the couch.

Vivi's calm and cold reaction was a sight to behold. Her features remained composed, her posture regal, and her voice measured, but beneath it all, there was a simmering fury that could not be ignored.

"All the money we paid for acting classes paid off, didn't it?" Vivi took a step toward her with confidence and then turned her head, glancing up the stairs. "Did you get that?"

"It's the scoop of the year. Of course, I did."

Like he could sense what was going on, Nathan stood up and then pushed Coco out of the way, running toward the door. As he swung it open, security pushed him back inside and grabbed him by his elbows, restraining him.

Coco looked up, seeing the woman with the camera coming down the stairs.

"You bitch." Coco lunged toward Vivi. "You can't film us secretly."

Another member of security grabbed Coco and restrained her.

Vivi shook her head. "She's a reporter. She can do whatever she wants, and I already gave her access to be here for the party."

Reporter Robin Callahan made her way downstairs, still pointing her camera at Coco.

Vivi approached Robin. "Thank you for believing me and coming all the way to Europe for your scoop."

"No, thank you for sending a private jet. I got to fly first class." She smiled.

"That's thanks to Tate. He insisted." Vivi winked at me.

"Can I just say I'm a big fan?" Robin smiled at me.

"Did I mention I am the favorite Blackwood sibling?" I gave Nathan a wink and then smiled at Robin. "Likewise. I enjoy your column."

"How can you do this to me?" Coco croaked suddenly and burst into tears. "I'm having your baby!"

"If you really are pregnant and I'm the father," I took one step closer to her, "then I'll be there for it. But only once I've got cast-iron proof. Until then, you can go to hell for all I care."

"You will regret this. I will post your video everywhere," she screamed and thrashed while security held her. "Nathan, do something!"

"What do you want me to do?" He sighed. "All they have is you blabbing your mouth. They have nothing on me, so I don't care."

"Baby!" she gasped. "What—I thought we were in this together!"

The clinking of heels could be heard over the floor. "He is a master manipulator; I can see how even you would fall for it."

Both Nathan and Coco turned in shock at the unfamiliar voice in the room. Valesca Astor, formerly Ethan's fiancé, Nathan's current wife, and Vivi's cousin, stepped into the room. She had waited for the right moment to stick the last nail in their coffin.

"Val, think about what you're doing here!" Nathan panicked the moment he saw her.

Valesca's entrance was like a tempest. It definitely brought in the dramatic effect Vivi and I had wanted. When Vivi brought up this idea, I had little to no faith that it would work, but a scorned and betrayed woman was a woman with a mission. Valesca didn't appreciate the fact that he'd cheated on her, was going to divorce her, and split the money with Coco.

Her piercing gaze settled on Nathan, and a grim smile played on her lips. She swept past me and Vivi, her heels clicking sharply on the floor, and set a heavy folder on the coffee table, full of evidence of Nathan's illegal activities.

Nathan's smug expression faltered as he glanced at the incriminating documents. "Tell me you didn't, Valesca?" he stammered, trying to regain his composure.

Valesca's eyes were like twin glaciers, icy and unforgiving. They bore into Nathan with a frigid intensity, piercing through his feeble attempts to defend himself.

"Baby." He moved straight onto begging.

"Baby?" Coco yelled. "Who are you calling baby, you lying son of a bitch?!"

Valesca brought her hand up and flipped Nathan off. "Fuck. You."

Vivi walked over to Coco, raised her hand, and slapped Coco's cheek. The sound echoed through the room, and everyone remained silent.

"You!" Coco screamed at the top of her lungs.

"That's for sleeping with my cousin's husband while he has a baby at home."

Nathan shook his head violently and looked at Valesca with pleading eyes. "I swear to you, I was using her to get to our money. I did it for us. Trust me."

"Trust you?" Valesca laughed. "Who do you think you are talking to?! The only thing you ever did for me was drain my money and my trust fund. I am divorcing your ass and taking custody."

"I love you!" Nathan teared up. He had completely abandoned Coco.

Valesca's poise was unshakeable. Her back remained straight, her movements deliberate, and her expression an unreadable mask of determination. No words or begging cracked her.

She and Vivi exchanged determined looks. It was sort of admirable.

"You can find more reasons to put him in jail in there." Valesca pointed at the folder. "Do what you will with that as long as you get me some sort of retribution. I need the bastard to pay for ruining my reputation and my life."

"Got it." Vivi nodded and crossed her arms, staring at both Coco and Nathan with contempt.

Nathan was visibly shaken. He didn't expect things to go this badly for him. I had a feeling he thought he would get away with this if he wasn't directly involved, but Valesca turning on him was not a card he expected us to hold.

I had heard from Ethan that Valesca used to be a force to be reckoned with, the kind that could bring even the worst of enemies to their knees, and it left no doubt that she was a woman not to be trifled with.

In partnership with Vivi, those two had just what they needed to bury the bastards. I didn't even have to get involved.

"What about our kid?" Nathan let a tear fall.

Vivi took a step closer to Nathan with a scoff. "Are you two reading the same script?! No one is buying your crap. If you really cared about your children, you never would have blackmailed us in the first place."

"This, Nathan," Valesca's voice dripped with contempt, "is the end of your little game. Your deceit, your affairs, your underhanded dealings—they're all laid bare in this folder. I have been watching you, every move, every misstep, waiting for the day you fuck me over so I can shove this in your face."

Nathan swallowed hard, the color draining from his face. He had underestimated Valesca, thinking she was powerless without him.

Valesca continued, her tone becoming more forceful. "I have grown weary of your games. I've decided to cut my losses and reveal it all, expose every dirty secret you thought was hidden. I was gonna give it to the authorities, the media, and anyone else who will listen. But now this is even better. Your own enemies can have it. I don't give a shit."

The realization of his impending downfall washed over Nathan, his arrogance turning to desperation.

"Also." She turned to Vivi. "I cloned their phones this afternoon while they were fucking in my bathtub today. He was brazen enough to bring her to my house while I was taking Pilates classes." She glared at him for a moment, then reverted her attention to us. "There is no video of you two. They were bluffing."

Vivi let out a sigh of relief and then hugged Valesca. "Thank you!"

Valesca placed a hand around her shoulder and gave Nathan and Coco a chilling smirk. "I will bring down anyone who plays with an Astor."

"They really messed up." Vivi smiled, glancing at Coco who was biting her lower lip in rage.

"Please escort them out," I told security and then picked up the folder from the coffee table. "I have to send this to both the French and the US police and call my lawyers."

Nathan began cursing and trying to get the security to let him go.

The security personnel, undeterred by his outburst, continued their mission to escort him out of the house, paying no heed to his tantrum. The moment we all stepped outside, Coco saw both her and Nathan confessing to their crimes, broadcasted on the large screen by the DJ's booth. Everyone at the party looked at them in disgust and judgment.

They both thrashed and cursed even more as the security team finally removed them from the premises.

"The *Manhattan Herald* would be delighted to report on this. Thank you for the firsthand scoop." Robin extended her hand to shake mine.

I took her hand into both of mine for a shake. "Thank you for agreeing to do this. You really helped us out a lot."

Robin swooned on the spot. She almost said something but then glanced at Vivi and released my hand. "I guess congratulations are in order. Are you two official yet?"

Vivi glanced at me, unsure.

"We are." I stepped in and placed my arm around Vivi. "You can write that in as well. Give it a nicer spin, will ya?"

Robin nodded with a grin. "If you ever change your mind," she glanced at Vivi, "give me a call. I'll take him off your hands."

"He is not going anywhere soon." Vivi raised herself on her toes and placed a kiss on my lips.

Valesca rolled her eyes, but a soft smile curved across her face. "Well, I'm going to grab some champagne to celebrate my win. Anyone in?"

It was a unanimous yes.

Chapter 25

Tate

Six weeks later, Manhattan

Baby, hurry!" Vivi yelled for the third time.

"I'm coming!" I rushed to her, carrying the last of the helium balloons, and then placed them in the corner of the room by the marble columns and tied them around it.

The Astor's Upper East Side mansion was brought to life by the number of caterers, decorators, and the jazz band that was setting up in the corner stage of the entertaining room. Alice, Vivi's head of staff, was ordering the flower delivery boys around while simultaneously explaining to the butler where the presents would go.

Vivi's twenty-first birthday was the social event of the season, and considering the upcoming movie and her budding fame, everyone wanted an exclusive ticket to her private birthday party.

With Coco's upcoming charges, she was long gone from the house, which left the villa at Vivi's disposal. Vivi debated it and then made the decision to revive the mansion by holding her first and semi-private party birthday party here. All her new closest friends, the movie staff, and my family were invited.

"There, how does that look?" I asked.

She gave the balloons one last look and smiled. "It's perfect. Thank you for jumping in to save the day. I thought the room looked empty without them. I just think it's a nice touch to a birthday party even though the decorator disagreed with me."

"What kind of birthday party doesn't have balloons?"

She smiled like a little girl. "Exactly. So, thank you for running this errand last minute for me."

I grabbed her by the waist and then pinned her next to me. "All this party planning has kept you occupied for the last three days. I was going to jump on any opportunity to get some of the attention back."

She wrapped her arms around my neck and raised herself on her already high heels. "You'll have all of me back after midnight."

"Perfect." I leaned forward, pressing my lips to hers. "I look forward to it."

She clung to me, indulging in the kiss for a minute. "I'm so happy," she whispered over my lips. "My dad would have loved seeing the mansion get its life back."

I gently stroked the back of her hair and embraced her with both my arms, tighter. "You don't have to force anything you don't want to do. Your dad would be proud either way."

"I know, but this home feels too lonely and quiet."

I pressed a kiss on the top of her head. "You seemed okay these past few weeks."

"That's because you were here." She raised her head, giving me her most innocent look. "I've grown attached to you. Alice has grown attached to you."

I raised a brow. "Alice has grown attached to me eating her cookies. I've already gained five pounds."

"And my butler has grown attached to you too."

I shook my head. "No, I have grown attached to the fact you grew up with a butler."

"I like having you here." She became anxious for a moment, and her cheeks flushed as they usually did when she was overthinking.

"What are you hinting at?" I brushed a loose strand of her styled bob behind her ear.

She took a deep breath and let the words out in one go. "I want you to move in with me." As soon as she said it, she changed her mind. "Is that too soon?"

The doorbell rang, and she jolted right out of my arms. "Just think about it, or don't. No pressure."

During the time we'd spent together, Vivi had gone softer, warmer, and more confident. Her laughter was more frequent, and she was more expressive.

I had grown too, so much so that I was starting to sound like Wade. Each conversation started with Vivi and I, and I mentioned her every chance I had. Time away from her seemed like wasted time. It was hard to part at night, and I had grown accustomed to waking up next to her every morning.

I clutched my chest, feeling my heart swell in warmth. The woman I loved just told me to move in with her. It was more than I could ever ask for.

I stood there watching her rush ahead, her butler trying to catch up as she went to greet her first guests.

Seconds later, Wade and Wren were welcomed in.

"Seems like we're early." Wade took a good second to look around before greeting me with a brotherly hug.

"Thank you for coming."

Wren walked in, walking by Vivi's side. They were immersed in a chat until the doorbell rang again. Wren joined me and Wade while waiting for the other guests.

"Look at you, all happy and stuff." Wren sidled up to me, a mischievous glint in her eye. "Your life seems disgustingly perfect. You've got the dream girl—an heiress at that—a successful movie shoot in Europe, and a whole new fan base after Robin's article in the *Manhattan Herald*. Tell me, what's it like to be the chosen one?"

"You don't get to complain." I pointed a finger at her. "Should I remind you what I had to put up with for weeks after you two got married? It was all newlywed talk for days."

She chuckled, shaking her head. "You are being dramatic. And you're getting your five minutes of fame now, aren't you?"

I shrugged. "I just got lucky, I guess."

She raised an eyebrow. "Lucky, huh? It's not like you're charming, talented, good-looking, and worked your ass off for this. Luck had nothing to do with it, Tate."

I couldn't help but smile at her witty banter. "Fine, what can I say? It must be the family genes."

She gave Wade a playful nudge. "That's why I married one of you."

I pressed my hands together. "And we are all very happy for you, but if you start again, I'll take my leave."

"I'm sorry." She laughed. "But seriously, Tate, you and Vivi make a hell of a couple. I'm happy for you both."

I nodded, touched by her genuine words. "Thanks, Wren. It means a lot."

Wade waved his hand. "Now, enough of this mushy stuff. Let's get back to enjoying the party and giving Vivi a twenty-first birthday she won't forget."

"Absolutely."

Some time later, the entertaining room was filled with the rest of the film cast that were invited to the party. Among them was Jeremy, the new leading man. Right after getting back to New York, Josie, Giles, and I worked hard to find a replacement for Vaughn, and with Carrie's recommendation, we found Jeremy, who was a new actor on the scene but had played Joel even better than Vaughn. We worked overtime to reshoot all Vaughn's scenes in New York, and a lot of extra effort was put in to pull it off, but lucky for us, Jeremy was more than willing to prove himself and help us out. The cast grew to like him a lot better than they did Vaughn.

With all the time spent together, the whole film crew had gotten close, and Vivi was accepted wholeheartedly, unlike when she was under Coco's influence.

The party had officially begun. Vivi greeted friends with hugs and kisses, her laughter filling the room. It was easy to see she was happier than ever.

The more I watched her, the more impatient I was to tell her my answer.

"Happy birthday, Vivi! It's about time we meet officially." Ethan and his wife Elizabeth arrived as well. Vivi insisted on inviting them, and I was more than happy she wanted to include everyone from my family in her life.

She shyly greeted both of them with a hug. "Thank you. It's a pleasure to finally meet both of you."

Elizabeth stepped forward, handing Vivi a beautifully wrapped gift. "We've heard so much about you. Thank you for inviting us."

Vivi accepted the gift with a warm smile. "Thank you, Elizabeth. I can't wait to see what's inside."

Ethan leaned in and whispered, "You're in for a treat. Elizabeth has excellent taste."

I walked over to greet them, and Vivi quickly took the gift and ran off. She'd avoided me ever since she brought up the moving in question.

"Hey," I welcomed them. "Thanks for coming."

"She's lovely." Elizabeth smiled.

"I wasn't sure how you'd feel about it since she's an Astor," I admitted.

She shrugged it off. "I don't judge people based on their family, trust me. I wouldn't want people to judge me on mine."

"Neither do I," Ethan and I said at the same time, both thinking about Nathan.

"Have you heard back from the lawyers yet?" I asked Ethan.

"Yes, they are working hard to make sure Nathan and Coco get jail time for attempting blackmail. Having all of the paperwork, thanks to Valesca, really helped out. We finally have something to bring down Nathan with," he answered.

Thankfully right after getting back to New York, I had pulled strings to get a blood test from Coco to see if she was pregnant. Like all the other lies she told, this was just another. She was never pregnant and had a fake pregnancy test to back up her lies that the police found when looking for more evidence. Vivi and I were relieved.

The doorbell rang once again. We all turned to each other and mouthed, "Flyn." Always fashionably late.

"Don't say anything now, but she is officially debuting Carrie as her girlfriend," I told them. "Let's be all cool about it."

"You say that as if you're not going to be the first to tease them." Ethan chuckled.

"Ah, but I made it happen, so I get a pass." I shrugged and took a champagne glass before heading to greet Flyn and Carrie.

Flyn had a gleeful smile on her face, arm in arm with Carrie. I couldn't help but feel a sense of accomplishment, knowing that I had played the part of breaking the ice and nudging them together.

Flyn was quick to greet Vivi, going in for a hug. "Happy birthday, gorgeous! You look absolutely stunning."

"Happy birthday." Carrie handed her a bouquet of pink peonies.

"Thank you." Vivi took it and then rushed off as soon as she saw me coming.

"Oh, oh what did you do now?" Flyn gave me a side-eye.

"She's just being shy." I smiled and glanced at Carrie. "Hey, I thought you'd be here way earlier with the rest of the cast."

Carrie paused before plastering a smile on her face. "I agreed to meet up with Flyn beforehand. Get some flowers for Vivi."

"Yes, Flyn is known for her deflowering." I avoided Flyn's hand right as she swung it at me. "I mean flower picking."

"Keep talking," Flyn warned me.

"I'm only happy for you two. If it wasn't for me, you'd still be thinking Carrie wasn't interested."

Flyn gave me an exaggerated eye roll and whispered to Carrie, "He's been milking that thing for weeks now. Just smile and nod."

"Come on, everyone is here." I led them to our little circle and then walked over to the podium where the band played.

Now that everyone was here, the atmosphere became more relaxed, and the conversation flowed easily.

I decided it was the perfect time to make a special announcement. With a nod and a smile, I asked the band to pause for a moment. The room hushed, and I glanced around, looking for Vivi to see if she was back. I didn't want her to miss this.

Just as she reentered the room, I raised my glass and called for everyone's attention. "Ladies and gentlemen, siblings, if I could have your undivided attention for just a moment. Today, we celebrate a very special occasion, as we gather to wish a happy twenty-first birthday to the most incredible woman I have ever met."

There was a chorus of cheers and applause as I continued. "I won't bore you with a long speech, but I do want to say this to you." I turned toward Vivi. "I've had the privilege of knowing you and being a part of your life for a very little time, but even then, you've been nothing short of magical. As a producer who's a harsh critic and as a man, I don't say that lightly. So, here's to you, Vivi, on your twenty-first birthday.

May your days be filled with laughter, your nights with love, and your years with success and happiness. I love you."

The room filled with the clinking of glasses and more cheers, but Vivi stared at me, tears gathering in her eyes. It was the first time she had heard me say *I love you*.

She rushed over to me, and the room erupted in applause as she hugged me tightly.

With her in my arms, I decided it was the perfect time to address the issue she'd been avoiding ever since she sprung it on me.

I gently pulled away from the embrace, looking into her eyes. "I have an answer for you." I brushed a thumb over her lips as she smiled. "I'd be more than happy to move in with you."

Her eyes glinted with excitement. She tossed her arms around me, hugging me, this time even tighter, her voice choked with emotion. "I love you, Tate."

"I love you more."

Chapter 26

Tate

Nine months later, Cannes Film Festival

The Cannes Film Festival.

The event was every bit of a dazzling whirlwind of glamour and prestige as one might expect. For the first time in my life, the nerves were eating me up on the inside. I had made it. Mom would have been so proud.

As I stood on the red carpet with the lights flashing and the excited chatter of the crowd in the background, I couldn't help but feel like I was living a dream. The entire experience was surreal. I had imagined a moment like this over a million times, and nothing compared to the real deal.

I tilted Joel's movie, *"Launching a Legacy,"* to tie in with Wren's bestselling book *"Legacy,"* but neither of us expected the whole thing to go viral. The whole world was suddenly interested in Joel Blackwood and his legacy.

The movie made its debut after a lot of hard work and dedication, and while I wanted it to be a success, I never expected things to come this far.

In the overwhelming noise and blinding lights, I felt the comforting grip on my hand.

Vivi was walking the red carpet with me, hand in hand in a long, white gown, gathering everyone's attention. The crowd loved her, and she was a natural.

Despite her worries that she wouldn't be able to handle the fame, she managed to stay grounded and calm throughout everything.

Her presence by my side filled me with a sense of pride and happiness I doubted the cameras could capture.

The red carpet was a sea of flashing cameras and enthusiastic fans as we walked along. The press had gathered in full force, eager to capture everything. I couldn't help but smile as I waved at the photographers, trying to soak in every moment.

The rest of the cast was walking right behind, taking pictures and giving interviews. Flyn was standing right next to Carrie, posing for the cameras.

Flyn glanced at me for a moment, winking at me before returning her attention to the photographers.

I calmed down. Having Flyn with me here as support was also comforting. She kept joking about one day joining me on the red carpet, only to have her be here nine months later. Life was unpredictable.

As we walked inside, I could still hear the muffled camera flashes and the shouts from the crowd. The atmosphere was electric, and the excitement was infectious. The response we had received from the audience during the screening of the movie earlier this week was overwhelming, and now the movie was nominated for the Jury Prize.

As we ventured farther into the venue, the Grand Palais des Festivals, the enormous auditorium was packed with the who's who of the film industry. I was in the same room with a lot of great people. The Jury Prize was one of the most prestigious awards at Cannes, and the possibility of winning it was almost too incredible to contemplate. I was happy to just be nominated.

Vivi squeezed my hand, her eyes filled with a mix of excitement and nerves.

"I can barely stand on my feet," she whispered as we were led to our seats. "I'm too excited."

"Me too. I can't believe we're here."

"I can't believe we made it either," Vivi whispered, her eyes shining with emotion. "We are nominated too. How did this happen in a few months?"

I held her trembling fingers in my hand and brought them up, placing a kiss on the top of her knuckles. "I am surrounded by amazing people who made this happen."

She rested her head against my shoulder. "I'm so proud of you. You've come a long way."

I pressed a kiss on her temple. "I couldn't have asked for a better partner, on and off the screen. Whatever happens, this movie is already a success, if you ask me."

"I love you," she mouthed as the rest took their seats and the award show started.

Lots of nerve-wracking moments later, the presenter began announcing the winners. The anticipation in the room was intense. With each category that passed, I couldn't help but feel a growing sense of anxiety. The Best Actor award went to a talented actor from another movie, and the Best Director award followed, but it wasn't until they announced the winner of the Jury Prize that my heart felt like it might explode.

The drumrolls echoed in my head.

"Launching a Legacy."

As the movie was pronounced as the recipient of the Jury Prize, the room erupted into applause and cheers. I paused in pure shock as I felt an overwhelming rush of emotion. I looked at Vivi, who was teary-eyed and smiling.

I rose and hugged her, then welcomed her and all of the cast to join me on stage.

As we made our way to the stage to accept the award, the world seemed to blur around us. The cheers from the audience, the flashing cameras, and the feeling of accomplishment all combined into a surreal moment. I could hardly believe this was happening.

Receiving the Jury Prize was a tremendous honor, a testament to the dedication and passion of the entire cast and crew. I allowed everyone to step up to the microphone and say something, including Director Giles. When it was finally my turn, the silence became overwhelming. I leaned toward the microphone.

"I feel like everything was said and all the gratitude was expressed through all my colleagues here. I'm absolutely grateful to everyone. But standing here, receiving this prize is life-changing, and this moment is not mine alone. I want to share it with someone really dear to me."

The stage lights reflected in my eyes as I reached into my pocket and took out the box. "I was going to do this after the festival, whether we won or not but ... Vivi." I turned to her, my voice filled with nervousness. "Tonight is a night of dreams coming true, and I can't imagine a more perfect moment to ask you something."

Her eyes widened, and a hint of curiosity mingled with surprise played across her features. The world around us seemed to blur as I got down on one knee.

The room echoed in gasps.

"I know this is not very subtle, but from this moment on, I want to share each and every success with you, and I can't imagine the rest of my life without you by my side. Will you marry me?"

Tears welled up in her eyes, and her hand flew to her mouth in astonishment. Another collective gasp echoed throughout the room. Time stood still as we waited for her response.

With trembling lips and tears glistening in her eyes, Vivi nodded vigorously. "Yes, yes!"

The room erupted into applause and cheers, and I slipped the ring onto her finger.

* * *

As the night drew to a close and the exhaustion of the day's events began to set in, Vivi and I sat in the quiet corner on the balcony overlooking the city. The lights of the French Riviera glittered beyond the windows of the other hotels. She was nestled in my arms, playing with the ring on her finger as we sat in silence.

"Tate," Vivi broke the stillness of the night first.

"Hm?" I glanced down at her.

She held her finger up, the ring glinting on it. "This means we have to do a wedding, right?"

"Are you changing your mind?" I intertwined our fingers together.

"No." Her voice filled with vulnerability. "I just remembered that neither of us can share this with our parents. It's times like these when I miss them the most."

Touched by her vulnerability, I held her tighter. "I do too, Vivi. But you know, in a way, they are here with us. They shaped us into who we became, which is how we found each other."

"You are such a romantic sometimes." She chuckled, but her voice was choked up with emotions.

With a hint of playfulness in her eyes, Vivi then changed her tone. "You know, Tate, I never would have guessed we'd end up back here, getting engaged on the French Riviera, the very place we met."

I chuckled. "I thought it was too good of an opportunity to surprise you when I planned to propose to you, though I surprised myself when I proposed on stage. I got swept away by my emotions."

The hotel room had been set up beforehand with rose petals and candles for our return after the event; little did I know I'd already be engaged by the time I got here. Vivi was laughing for ten minutes after seeing the setup I'd abandoned to propose on stage.

"Spontaneity suits you," Vivi teased. "It's what I love about you."

Unable to contain my affection, I leaned in and whispered, "How about we go back inside, finish that bottle of wine, and continue where we left off?"

Her face broke into a radiant smile. "We already ruined every inch of this hotel room that was covered with petals."

I smirked. "Not the bathtub. We never made it there."

She turned around, wrapping her arms around me, and kissed me. "Lead the way then."

Epilogue

Six months later

A little bird told me ...

Well, well, well, dear readers of the Manhattan Herald! Hold on to your fascinators and roll out the red carpet, because *Tate Blanchard* and *Viviana Astor* have officially tied the knot! *That's right, the charismatic pair, whose love story has had more twists and turns than their own movie, are now hitched. Seems I have to say goodbye to my crush on my favorite Blackwood heir.*

The family was all together this weekend to celebrate their wedding, and it didn't go without a few surprises for the public, and I have the official scoop.

Before we get into the juicy details, we have to mention our favorite actress, Vivi, who looked breathtaking. She walked down the aisle in her late mother's dress, and no I'm not talking about Coco Astor, who turned out to be her evil stepmother. This love story had plot twists that could make Cinderella jealous.

On the receiving end, Tate Blanchard looked sharp in a tailored suit that screamed Hollywood heartthrob as he said his vows to Vivi.

His siblings, Wade and Flyn, were right by his side, dressed impeccably. And what about Ethan Blackwood, you ask? You'll find out in a little bit.

The ceremony was nothing short of a fairy tale. It took place in a secluded garden venue, tucked away from prying eyes and flashing cameras. The scent of blooming flowers and the gentle hum of chirping birds set the stage for a day filled with love and laughter and a little bit of drama.

Elizabeth Blackwood and Wren Blanchard both brought some unexpected guests to the event. The twist? They both revealed matching baby bumps. Seems like we are getting some additions to our favorite celebrities.

Tate and Vivi's reactions were nothing short of heartwarming. They couldn't stop smiling, and the collective "awws" from the guests made it a moment to remember. Tate even made a charming speech, declaring that their new additions would be cherished and adored, much like the legacy he'd been so inspired to honor in his award-winning film.

Speaking of legacy, the absence of Vivi's beloved father, Jasper Astor, was noticed, and Ethan Blackwood stepped in to give the radiant bride away. It was a heartwarming sight to behold.

We love the unbreakable bond these found-family siblings share.

Another unexpected guest was Valesca Astor herself. Yes, you heard that right. It appears that she's been welcomed back into the fold, making this wedding a true family affair!

The socialite and her past antics have left more than a few eyebrows raised and gossip columns buzzing. But, dear readers, it seems that love and forgiveness prevailed in the end, as she took her place among the wedding guests.

This brings us to the black sheep of the family who's been hanging around the Blanchard-Blackwood-Astor clan for far too long—Nathan Valletta. If you've been living under a rock, he has made quite the enemy out of his half-siblings and even earned himself a nice jail sentence for his charming attempts at blackmail and some other shady business.

Well, dear readers, it appears the dark clouds have lifted, and the skies are finally clear. The question on everyone's minds is: Will we ever hear another peep out of Nathan? Let's all cross our fingers and hope that this particular bird won't be chirping anytime soon!

With this, I wrap up the Manhattan Fairytale. Despite the unexpected surprises, absent family members, and old drama, the couple's love shone through, brighter than the lights of Times Square. Cheers to Tate and Vivi, may your love story continue to be as captivating as any scandal in the gossip columns!

Written by your resident gossip columnist,
Robin Callahan

About the Author

EJ St. Claire is a gifted and passionate romance writer whose captivating stories will make your heart race and pulse quicken. EJ is an English major turned author with a deep love for language and storytelling, and has spent countless hours perfecting the art of crafting memorable characters and enthralling plots. An award-winning writer, EJ draws inspiration from life's great adventures and misadventures from a lifetime of reading, traveling, and experiencing the world.

EJ's literary works have readers eagerly anticipating the chance to delve into the world of passion, love, and romance that EJ has created. While Readers can be assured that this talented author brings a wealth of experience and expertise to their craft. When not writing, EJ can be found curled up with a good book, sipping endless cups of tea, and enjoying the company of their beloved pets and spouse.

www.ejstclaire.com

Coming Soon

www.legacyunhinged.com

Also By EJ St. Claire

Legacy Book Series

Legacy Undone

Legacy Uncensored

Legacy Unscripted

Legacy Unhinged

www.ingramcontent.com/pod-product-compliance
Lightning Source LLC
Chambersburg PA
CBHW060150180626
46813CB00007B/2692